THE CIPHER OF KAILASH

RAHUL RAI

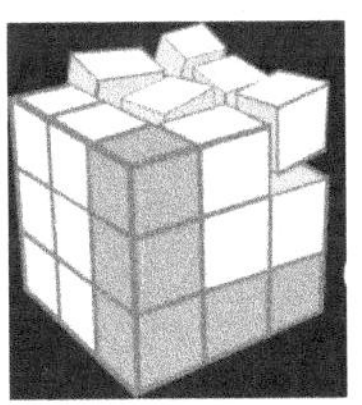

LOGIPUB SERVICES
(Since 2012)

By the same author –

The Myth of Hastinapur

Published by:

LOGIPUB SERVICES

1404, Land Craft Golf Link Society NH-24, Ghaziabad - 201009

ISBN: 978-8-1937-7155-6
Price: 310.00

CONTENTS

"The ghastly sound, like the raucous wheeze of rotten lungs, emanated from a distance. Its repugnance instilled fear in the hearts of even the wildest of creatures. The hyenas feasting on the dead scurried towards shelter; their snouts dripping fresh blood, and their bellies still half-fed. The wolves bolted towards their den; their tails cleanly tucked between their legs. The lioness trembled in fear; her eyes tightly shut. She clutched at her cubs, who whined softly in her tight embrace. It was pitch dark - darker than the heart of a demon; darker than the tongue of Kaali. One could barely make out his own hands in front of him; let alone the bow and arrows. And in that gloom, Lakshman stood in rapt attention, holding his breath. He closed his eyes and tried to locate the source of the frightful sound. Straightening his body, he reached for his quiver. Five arrows left his bow in quick succession. The wheeze changed to a low groan as the arrows hit their mark. The whole forest thundered as the *Rakshashas* ululated in agony. Tadka had a hard time fleeing Lakshman's rage," the villager continued, excitedly spinning a story for the group.

The sage raised his fiery red eyes. He was always amused by the power of storytelling. Woven out of facts, or simply figments of imagination, stories held a lot of power over people. 'Whatever you do, make sure you have a great story to tell,' his master used to say. Stories had the ability to make the profane sacred; to catapult ordinary humans to the stature of divinity, or to push them deep into a muck of evil. He knew many stories which had reached epic proportions, and had inspired countless generations; stories which were modified into titbits to suit different tastes, while preserving their core. His, was one such story.

'A thousand men were killed, and another thousand waited to be slain by his axe. Soldiers swarmed in droves, only to see their bodies being dismembered by the onslaught of the sage. He fought without mercy, for a month, against the whole army of Mahismati,' he remembered hearing about himself.

'His axe has been blessed by the Gods. Death won't cross his path until it protects him.' There were many other tales floating about him.

A loathsome *Rakshashi*, Tadka was currently ruling one of the largest territories in the whole of *Aryavarta*. Along with her loyal and fierce soldiers, she had struck fear into the hearts of people in the adjoining kingdoms. Many proud *Aryavarta* kings have been killed by her hands, and several towns had been ransacked by her army. People from nearby villages had chosen to migrate, rather than live in constant fear of her barbarity. Those who remained had to face the brunt of double taxation; a part of their produce went to their kings, while a part of it was forcefully taken away by the *Rakshashas*. The forests, which were once dotted by many *ashrams* owing to its serenity and solitude, were now deserted by the sages. Only one tribe flourished in those forests now: The *Rakshashas*. No one was prepared to reside in her ever-increasing sphere of influence, aptly named Tadka *van*. Injured, maimed and gouged - many *rishis* had approached him in the past with the request to remove the danger. But he was bound by an oath. Kshatriya blood was the only crimson stain his axe bathed in.

Tadka *van*, a densely forested area, suited the battle techniques of the *Rakshashas*. While other *Aryavarta* kingdoms were used to warring in open, barren battlefields, the *Rakshashas* were adept at guerrilla tactics and camouflage. They fought in small groups and employed minimal weaponry. Their heavy muscular bodies, bereft of any armour, provided the much-needed agility against their opponents. Wielding crude weapons, which included thick branches of trees, they annihilated even the most trained battalions in seconds. Many kings fought and surrendered to the scourge of the *Rakshashas*.

It was a scorching day, and a long journey lay ahead. Being short of height, the long and thick gleaming axe looked peculiar on his shoulder. It seemed too heavy to be carried by an ordinary human, but he seemed to hold it with ease. He was used to moving with short, quick steps, without breaking pace, but the conversation he had overheard slowed him down. He decided to hear more about Lakshman whom the villager had referred to. The axe had to wait.

***

A terrible drought had prevailed over the past few years, and had rendered the fields of nearby villages barren. The villagers tried various methods to conserve water, along with the local priest's multiple calls to the rain Gods - but to no avail. While nature had decided to make them starve, it didn't deter the local chieftain from collecting taxes from the poor villagers. Suketu, the chieftain, wreaked havoc on the farmers who requested him to waive the year's rent.

"Any man worth his salt, pays his dues. One who refuses to do so, bears no dignity and is unfit to live. There is no sin if he is exploited as an animal," he used to say.

Burning houses, abducting children and women, beating farmers to death - Suketu's gang committed felonies freely to serve the whims of their master and collect rent, while the chief remained deaf to the hue and cry of his fellow villagers.

The villagers had become accustomed to such sporadic events of violence, but a few days earlier, things had taken a turn for the worse. It happened during one of those colder than usual mornings. The villagers tried to remain snuggled in bed for as long as possible; their deep slumber triggered by a sudden chill in the air. They dragged themselves lazily to the fields, cursing their luck as the sun's rays tried to break through the fog. It has been many days since they had found any respite from their hard work. Without any rains, they had to constantly protect the newly sown seeds from birds throughout the day. It was the shrill cry of a teenager that shook them from their reverie. The villagers ran towards the boy, who looked petrified by the scene in front of him. Many fainted, while others stopped in their tracks on witnessing the horror. At least twenty charred bodies were lying together in a field, blackened with ash and smoke. Seeing how the bodies lay curled, it looked like they had been burnt alive. Small, half-burnt pieces of cloth lying near their faces suggested their mouths had been stifled before they had been set on fire. The bodies of three children, aged less than seven, were also lying among the dead. The smell of their charred flesh hung heavily in the air. A warning to pay rent without delay was scrawled on a plaque. The morning chill, it seemed, entered the spines of the helpless villagers.

The villagers dreaded looking into the eyes of Suketu or his gang. They were quite aware of the predicament of farmers who had tried to stand against him in the past. But seeing the bodies of their friends and families, burnt beyond recognition, exposed their absolute vulnerability against a wretched monster.

"We have to choose between living under the constant threat of death, or seeking Ram's help," one of the village elders at the scene spoke after a few minutes. The others were still frozen in their places. The shock was too much for them to digest.

"And we need to act fast," said another. Few in the crowd nodded their heads at the suggestion.

For the next few hours, the villagers busied themselves in cremating the charred remains of their brethren as per the religious rites.

Towards the end, the whole village had warmed up to the suggestion of discussing their misfortunes with Ram. The village chose a few young adults for this task. They left for his *ashram* after offering their prayers to the dead.

"He hasn't wielded his axe in years," said one, as the group started for Ram's *ashram*.

"When has such horror been played before your eyes?" said the youngest of the group. He had lost his brother in this mishap. Wiping his tears, he said, "He would certainly respond to our plight."

It took the group a couple of days to reach Ram's *ashram*. They were welcomed by the sight of students practicing with deadly weapons. Seeing so many trained warriors in one place, who were quite renowned for their righteousness, calmed their nerves a bit. They watched with interest as students engaged in duels, challenging each other to their limits. Ram waved at them and asked them to wait since he was busy teaching his students.

Once the routine practice was over, Ram walked over to the villagers. His blood boiled as he listened to their plea for justice. He could empathise with their confusion over the prevailing emotions which were driving their thoughts – the grief over the gruesome death of their loved ones was fighting against the absolute fear they felt for those living.

"There is no greater crime than killing an innocent," Ram said, running his fingers over the deep scar on his right arm, "I will make him pay for his sins."

Ram closed his eyes, forcing himself to meditate. He needed some time alone to digest the grief portrayed before him. Also, he didn't want to appear weak before the villagers.

'Never show your tears to others,' his master used to say, 'They portray your truest emotions and expose the most vulnerable parts of your personality.'

He dismissed the assembly with a wave of his hand. The villagers were already getting late. They wanted to reach their village before it got too dark. After a modest offering of a few sacks of grains, they left for their homes.

Early the next morning, Ram reached the banks of river Ganga. For many years, he never missed a single day coming here. He waddled waist-deep into the water. Balancing his weight on one leg while raising the other, he prayed with his eyes closed, facing the sun. After a few minutes, he returned after finishing his bath.

Ram was quite agile for his age. Years of training at the feet of Shiva, coupled with a disciplined lifestyle, had helped him immensely to maintain his athletic physique. For an hour, his body breezed through the movements of various *asanas*. Beads of sweat shimmered on his forehead as the sun rose above the horizon. He looked behind him and found the blade glistening in the light. He practiced against an imaginary target using his axe for a couple of hours, dexterously cutting through the air; his feet moving like a trained acrobat.

"You will taste blood after a long time," he muttered, dipping the axe in the river and finally beginning his long journey on foot.

***

Ram's red eyes met the hot sun as it reached its zenith. The streets were almost deserted due to the heat, and even the insides of the thatched huts were unbearable. People sat in small bands at the doorway, which was protected by the long shadow cast by the roof on the ground. He reached the group, who were discussing the incidents involving Tadka, and asked for some water to wet his parched throat.

"But his elder brother is a pillar of calmness," the conversation continued, "Without Ram, it would not have been so easy for Lakshman. He seems quite quick-tempered."

The sage's curiosity was piqued at the mention of his namesake. He knew Tadka was no ordinary *Rakshashi*. Supported by her competent sons, Subahu and Mareech, along with her clan, she was fierce and could make mincemeat of an entire battalion of trained soldiers. Therefore, anyone throwing a challenge to her was worth discussing.

"Who are these people that you speak of?" the sage inquired as the afternoon sun became intolerable. He emptied a jug of water over his head.

A couple of villagers looked up at the short, well-built Brahmin. They had to shield their eyes to catch a glimpse of him. Since the sun beamed furiously from the opposite side, the sage's burning eyes, his flowing white beard, and his battle-ready face glowed under the reflection of the axe. Sweat, intermingled with water, flowed freely across his naked chest and streaked through a deep red scar that ran from his right shoulder to the edge of his ribs on the left - almost like the mark of a *janeudhari* (one who wears the sacred thread) was embossed on him. There were various other deep cuts and bruises across his body, indicating his years spent battling fearless warriors. A *rudraksh* string necklace adorned his right arm like a bracelet, while he wielded the axe using his left hand; his trained fingers clasping it tightly. A worn-out lionskin was firmly wrapped around his waist. Though old, it had a clean look to it. Sages were supposed to take their personal hygiene seriously.

"The Princes of Ayodhya," the lone woman in the group stated, "Lakshman and Ram." She closed her eyes in reverence as she uttered their names. With her palms pressed against each other in a respectful *pranam*, she started chanting Ram's name. The sage was not surprised. Many a time, he had seen such devotion from ordinary villagers for their kings and saviours. Even his name was shown similar veneration in many villages throughout the country.

"They have killed most of her fellowmen," the woman continued, "They are still so young. Finally, Ayodhya has something to boast about."

The sage looked towards the sun, trying to gauge the time. Memories of Surya flooded his senses. There was still some distance left to cover. He resumed his journey, noting that he had to quicken his pace to stay on schedule. He wanted to finish his work by dusk.

***

"Save us from Tadka," he remembered the cries of a group of ascetics who had come to the royal court of Dakshin Kosal, while he was on a visit.

King Sukaushal had sent many expeditions, led by able generals, to kill Tadka, but none of them had succeeded. He looked helplessly towards his ministers for some sound advice, but none had anything to say. Ram sat quietly watching the proceedings.

"What I can offer you is a safe abode in my kingdom. Build your *ashrams*, bring your students, raise your family, and live peacefully in my kingdom for as long as you want. Kosal would always be indebted to you," he said at last.

"We have not come here to seek refuge, King. We are here to ask you to perform your duty by protecting our lands," one of the sages in the group intoned in a commanding voice.

Sukaushal searched his memory as he looked towards the sage. His face looked familiar. It was Nimishmantra, whose grandfather had served in the royal court of Dakshin Kosal. Quite early in his life, he had decided to take *sanyas*. He had been taught by some of the most famous sages of *Bharatvarsh*. Sukaushal had the good sense not to argue with a sage of his stature.

"The whole army of Dakshin Kosal is at your command, sage, but you must be aware of the number of times I have tried to get rid of this menace. If you wish, I can send the ableist warriors to accompany you to the forest, but judging by our past experiences, I don't see think it will be a wise decision," Sukaushal answered humbly.

The *rishis* knew Sukaushal was not lying, nor did they doubt his intent. Many kingdoms found themselves helpless in front of Tadka and her army. They looked towards each other and decided to leave.

"It seems we have to find a way on our own." It was Nimishmantra again who stood up in a huff.

The king rose from his throne and walked towards the group to bid them farewell. "Each one of you is welcome to build your *ashram* in my kingdom," he said with the utmost sincerity. The fearsome Tadka had at least one less kingdom to worry about.

A few months later, another piece of news reached King Sukaushal's court. Sage Vishvamitr had asked him to visit a village close to Tadka *van*. A sage by the name of Nimishmantra, who had been a citizen of Dakshin Kosal, was killed by a rabid group of *Rakshashas* who'd attacked his *ashram* a few days ago, and burned it to ashes. Most of his students also belonged to the same region. Sukaushal was asked by Vishvamitr to identify those who were killed, and to carry their bodies back to their families.

***

Ram was still a few hours away from his destination. The mention of Tadka had opened the floodgates of his memories. Surya Shrestha returned to haunt him. A Brahmin by birth, Surya had been one of his favourite students. Every year, Ram took a fresh batch of students under his tutelage. The initial selection criterion was simple – Ram only accepted children of Brahmins as his pupils. Quite early in his life, he had observed how absolute power corrupted the minds of kings and princes. The priests who belonged to the Brahmin class provided legitimacy to that power, and in return, received favours from kings in the form of alms, jewels, farmlands and employment in royal courts. With no army or kingdom of their own, these priests, though venerated for their knowledge, had to depend on kings for their survival. Ram decided to train these priests in the art of warfare and military strategies, and urged them to carve an independent destiny for themselves, free from the influence of Kshatriya chiefs. That way, when the time came, they could muster the courage to stand against the despotic rulers.

The selected pupils underwent one of the most unique learning programs designed for Brahmins in the entire country. While Kshatriyas had multiple avenues to learn the art of warfare, Ram's *ashram* was the only one in the country to impart that knowledge to Brahmins. Ram was a strict taskmaster and an accomplished teacher. His ways attracted many families, residing in even the remotest of locations, to send their children to his *ashram*. Most *ashrams* stressed the importance of learning the Vedas and other religious texts, contrary to which Ram turned his students into fearless warriors - a group of self-sufficient Brahmins ready to stand and fight for the continuity of *Sanatan Dharm* and its ideals. Once their training was over, these Brahmins returned to their hometowns and settled there, acting as a bulwark of justice and truth.

Like many students, Surya had come to learn archery from him. But gaining Ram's confidence was not easy. He was known for his temper and followed a rigorous training schedule. A descendant of Bhrigu – the son of the creator, Brahma; fathered by one of the *saptarshis* Jamdagni; the student of the supreme destroyer, Shiva; revered as the sixth avatar of Vishnu; the one who slew the mightiest king in the history of *Bharat*; slayer of numerous brave Kshatriya clans - Ram was no ordinary Brahmin. To become his disciple, one had to prove his worth through various tests. The difficulty of these tests increased with each level. Only one out of a hundred people survived the tests, and only a tenth were able to complete the entire course successfully. However, Surya proved to be a student of exceptional abilities. Since day one, he had excelled in all the tasks. Everyone knew he would bring glory to the *ashram* in the future.

The students were required to follow three tenets for life: 'Don't depend on alms, make yourself productive' was the first. Unlike those Brahmins who joined temples as priests or practiced penance, or opened *ashrams* to further religious studies, these Brahmins tilled lands, tended to cows, or joined professions like the other local Vaishyas. They busied themselves with looking after the needs of the local populace. Few kingdoms adopted the practice of appointing these Brahmins as *lokayuktas*, one who is appointed by the people. These *lokayuktas* served as a watchdog to ensure the local regime conducted its business in accordance with *Niti*, *Dharm* and *Nyay*.

'Rule of law is necessary for the prosperity of the subjects' was the second tenet to be followed. If the local chieftain dithered from his *Dharm,* or performed unscrupulous acts against his subjects, or turned into a tyrant, the students of Ram brought forth their well-studied art of negotiation into play. They implored the despot to mend his ways, held councils for meting advice, or threatened him with dire consequences to make the king and his ministers realize their mistakes.

'A king is a trustee of the people. Acting against the very people who put their trust in him is the biggest treachery,' Ram used to say. If all efforts at reconciliation failed, they mobilised the masses to revolt against the regime. Many Kshatriya kings around *Bharatvarsh* faced the wrath of Ram's students. It was during those times that the world witnessed the effects of Ram's training - an unforgiving, principled war machine, with his army of villagers plied with rudimentary weapons, rained havoc on the forts of mighty kings. A successful revolution was the norm for students of Ram. Post dethroning the oppressor, they assumed the authority of the king until the people found an effective ruler for their kingdom.

"No prisoners. Spare none," Ram bellowed at Surya during one of the mock drills. This was the principle he had followed throughout his life. If the first two tenets failed in bringing equanimity to the kingdom, its ruler didn't deserve a speck of kindness, and ending his life was the only befitting punishment. Ram was quite impressed by Surya's focus, persistence, and keenness to learn. He could see an adept general in the making.

For four years, Surya rigorously practiced under Ram's patronage. Every day, the students and their teacher followed an unwavering routine. They woke up at four in the morning, and practiced weaponry and martial arts till the sun was about to set on the horizon. Only meal breaks were allowed during that time. Weary from the day's drill, the pupils and the teacher sat together for a long dinner, interspersed with discussions around the life and its perils. The discussions were just as enlightening as the lessons held during the day. Various religious texts and their interpretations were discussed at length until Ram chose to retire for the night, only to repeat the same schedule the following day. The students' intelligent, but impressionable minds quenched their thirst at Ram's feet. Except for two months in summer, the *ashram* allowed no breaks or holidays.

"You poor souls find this schedule hard to follow for just four years? I have followed this all my life," Ram used to tell them.

On his last day at the *ashram*, Surya came to his teacher and requested a *Guru Dakshina*. Ram smiled, "Bestow this earth with the justice it seldom receives. Protect the Brahmins, their *ashrams,* and the tenets of *Sanatan Dharm*. You can do no greater service than proving yourself to be better than me. Try to surpass my reputation, and I shall be satisfied with knowing that I have taught you well."

The escapades of Surya reached Ram's ears in the coming years. Unmerciful against *Rakshashas*, dacoits and looters, Surya became the protector of the ascetics. Aided by his band of loyal soldiers, he kept many *ashrams* safe from all calamities. Assuming a large tract of forest under his command, which expanded exponentially, he created an expanse of serenity. Various *ashrams* mushroomed around the area owing to his efforts. A few of the surrounding villages regarded him as the avatar they had been waiting for. They erected temples to commemorate his acts. Ram was amused when he heard such stories. 'Too many avatars are present on Mother Earth at the same time,' he thought.

"We are oath-bound to not hurt anyone who has done no harm. But why is there so much stress on protecting only Brahmins and their *ashrams*?" asked one of Surya's followers, once. He too was a student of Ram.

"For the continuity of *Sanatan Dharm*," said Surya, mulling over his friend's concern. "It is through these *ashrams* that life-skills get transferred to our society at large. *Ganit, bhugol, rasayan shastra*, tenets of *Dharm*, military skills, and other significant aspects of life are learned here. It is at a temple of vocational training where a student learns to become self-sufficient.

A society is built upon certain rules which the majority chooses to accept. Those rules might look peculiar to an outsider, but they make sense to the community which follows it. In the absence of a good teacher, it would become difficult to transfer these values to the next generation, which would put the very existence of our society into jeopardy. Our *ashrams* are the nodal points to ensure that the Aryan culture flourishes, and its values remain relevant for the coming generations.

Contrary to popular belief, our teacher, Ram, bears no hatred towards the Kshatriyas; rather, his hatred is directed towards kings with inflated egos, who are busy indulging in larger than life existences without sparing a single thought to the welfare of their subjects. The appropriation of culture can only happen on a full stomach. Starved subjects weaken the empire from within. Therefore, for the continuity of our *Dharm*, it is vital to protect the righteous Brahmins and to get rid of these pompous Kshatriyas."

"And this continuity is what the *Rakshashas* want to break?" asked a warrior from Surya's army.

Surya nodded in response. "Unless we can prevent them from breaking it."

Surya's name quickly caught people's attention as the lone crusader against the mighty *Rakshashas*. He was able to challenge demons who made even the large kingdoms feel helpless. Owing to his reputation, a lot of Brahmins started requesting his assistance to drive the *Rakshashas* out of their *ashram's* vicinity.

Sage Vishvamitr was one such Brahmin who sought Surya's help. He had employed many of Parshuram's students in the past for such expeditions. Whether it was killing a loathsome *Rakshasha*, or a wild beast which had become a man-eater, or protecting the border kingdoms from foreign attacks - Vishvamitr knew exactly where help would be readily available.

"Bring the sage in quickly. Why did you ask him to wait at the gates?" Surya asked the guard angrily, who had informed him about Vishvamitr's visit.

The guard lowered his head in guilt. "Don't just wait here," Surya bellowed.

"Wait, I will come with you," he added as an afterthought.

Surya hurried towards the gate and touched Vishvamitr's feet, asking for forgiveness for having made him wait.

"Surya, I have heard a lot about you," said Vishvamitr in his deep sonorous tone.

"It's all because of your blessings, *Brahmarshi*," said Surya, his voice cracking. Receiving praise from a sage of Vishvamitr's stature was indeed overwhelming.

"I have come here to ask you for a favour," stated Vishvamitr, following Surya inside.

"Sages of your stature don't ask for favours, *Brahmarshi*. They command puny mortals like me," Surya expressed with utmost gratitude.

"The whole *Aryavarta* is grateful for your service," Vishvamitr replied, before continuing, "I am here to ask you to help us, the sages, against the wrath of Tadka."

Surya looked at him, trying to ascertain if he had heard the right words. For years, no one had dared to challenge Tadka. She was beyond the reach of armies of almost every kingdom. Once his training at Ram's *ashram* had been completed, Surya had taken an oath to dedicate his life towards the protection of the sages' *ashrams* across the country. He knew that there would come a day, if he were still alive while following this arduous path, when this journey would bring him against Tadka. He didn't realize it would happen so soon.

"That is a huge responsibility, *Brahmarshi*. I shall be available to serve you at the earliest," said Surya earnestly.

"Don't do it just because I am asking for it. Tadka is more dangerous than what most people think," Vishvamitr warned, handing over an old torn parchment. There was some text scrawled on the bark of a dead tree. It looked like it was written in blood.

Surya read it out aloud. "We need to unite to destroy these temples of indoctrination which have mushroomed across the country. They try to chain and subjugate us. They view *Rakshashas* as a senile race to be wiped out from the face of the earth. They disrespect our cultural practices and demonise our kings and seers. One of the greatest kings of our times, Ravan, a half-Brahmin himself, is unfit to rule *Bharatvarsh* since his birth mother was a *Rakshashi*. The whole of *Aryavarta* is conspiring to have him killed. Why? Because they do not want to be ruled by someone whose blood is 'polluted' by the *Rakshasha* clan. This is now the sole purpose of our existence - to prevent this subjugation to 'Aryan rule'.

Right from childhood, the minds of the young are bathed in the cesspool of Aryan culture every day, at such *ashrams*, the so-called centre of knowledge. Let us prevent every seer, whom we can lay our hands on, from doing so. Let us also try to 'pollute' the pure Aryan blood with ours. When there is enough *Rakshasha* blood flowing through the veins of *Aryavarta*, no one would deny our rightful place. Then, Ravan will rule; not only the *Bharatvarsh*, but the whole world."

"Those are the words of Tadka, the current queen of territory as large as the city of Kashi. But her ambitions don't stop there," said Vishvamitr. The sage had predicted correctly. The city of Kashi was a vast area expanding over a few square kilometres. Since then, Tadka *van* had become the largest stronghold of the *Rakshasha* clan. The present size of Tadka *van* could subsume many Kashis.

Surya listened intently to what the seer had to say. He was already aware of the vicious plan of the *Rakshashas*. In his mind, winning against Tadka would be no small feat. It was time to render the greatest service a student could do for his teacher, to prove that his master had taught him right.

A few months later after Vishvamitr had left, Surya faced his nemesis, Tadka. He, along with his group of trained warriors, went deep into the forest in search of the *Rakshashi*.

Their plan was simple. First, they would discreetly find her hiding place and lie in wait without getting noticed until she undertook another planned attack. They would allow the attack to take place to not raise any suspicion. Meanwhile, they would regroup and wait for Tadka's return to unleash an ambush. The *Rakshashas* who remained alert throughout an attack, generally laid down their defences once it was over. Tired of all the killing and looting, they would look for some respite. It would be at this opportune moment that Surya and his band would commence their attack. Surprised by the sudden onslaught, they assumed that the *Rakshashas* would succumb to the might of their army.

With a plan in place, Surya and his group surreptitiously built their camps on the boundary of Tadka *van*. A month before, they had been able to locate the hiding place of Tadka. Every night, from then on, few from the group were sent to keep an eye on the activities of the *Rakshashas*, while the others patiently awaited the next attack to commence.

On one such moonless night, Surya and his group finally got a chance to face Tadka. They ambushed the settlement late at night. The *Rakshashas* had just returned from pillaging and destroying a nearby village and were sitting gregariously around a large bonfire whilst celebrating their success. The flames leapt high into the sky. *Soma* flowed freely, and most of them seemed to be in an inebriated state. Few sat on straw mats enjoying their meal, while most of them danced around the fire, hand in hand, singing at the top of their voices. Their chief, Tadka, had also joined the celebrations. She was moving from one group to another, serving wine from a large flask. The silence of the jungle was disrupted by the cacophony of their deep sonorous voices.

Surya's crew waited with bated breaths for their commander's orders.

They had surrounded the clearing. Their blood boiled on hearing the interloping cries of women and children, whom the *Rakshashas* had taken as prisoners. The archers took their positions behind heavy rocks and trunks, while the soldiers wielding spears climbed onto the trees. The sword bearers stood rigid, attentive to the enemy's movements, but the *Rakshashas* seemed to be lost in their revelry. Tadka, a curse to the kingdoms of *Aryavarta*, was about to be killed.

Surya fired the first arrow towards its target, which signalled the others to follow suit. It hit Tadka, who had been sitting with her sons after serving her companions, just below her neck. She whimpered in pain, trying to make sense of what had hit her. Most of the *Rakshashas* enjoying their drinks were not carrying any weapon on themselves at that time. Seeing their commander in anguish, they ran to their shelters to arm themselves, but in that instant, spears rained down from the skies, only to be followed by an assault of stones which were pelted by the soldiers occupying the treetops. In under a minute, a quarter of the group was dead. Before they could get any respite, the swordsmen came running and slashing through the clearing, killing men, women and children in hordes. Bodies piled on top of each other until even death lost count.

Tadka stood writhing in pain. Another arrow had pierced her back by then. She looked towards the direction from where the arrows were being fired from. Picking up a burning log, she ran towards the well-built man who seemed to be leading the forces. But her enemy had quick reflexes. In no time, he had buried two more shafts near her heart. However, these near-fatal wounds were not enough to break the stride of the giant of a *Rakshashi*.

In no time, she had closed ranks to engage Surya in a fistfight. She forcefully swung the log she was carrying, but Surya ducked quickly to avoid it. Grabbing a sword from his fellow men, Surya gave a wild swing and wounded Tadka's thighs. The *Rakshashi's* cry of pain shook the whole forest. Before she could regain her balance, Surya kicked her in the torso. With a loud thud, she fell in front of him. The arrows puncturing her body buried themselves deeper. Tadka bit her tongue from the pain and remained motionless on the ground for a few moments. The log had fallen from her hand and landed on a patch of dried leaves covering the forest ground.

"*Har Har* Mahadev," Surya bellowed, raising his sword above his head one last time. He aimed for Tadka's neck, but she dodged the attack at the last minute. His sword struck the hard ground instead. Surya tried to pull it out, but before he could, a hot strike to his shin caught him off guard. He tried to regain his posture, but another strike threw him off-balance.

Tadka stood holding the wooden log. Sparks flew as she began beating Surya to a pulp using all her strength, giving him no chance to recover or to fight back. The forest grounds were ablaze by then, and the fires were spreading fast. Tadka took hold of Surya's legs and started pulling him towards the centre of the clearing. Fear sank its icy grip deep into the hearts of the soldiers who saw their commander gasping for air. Surya tried to break free but the *Rakshashi* was too strong for him. With one swift movement, she threw him into the bonfire. Surya's screams reverberated through the forest and even the bravest of soldiers were shaken by his tragic end.

The *Rakshashas* gained confidence on seeing the courage of Tadka. The spearmen on top of the trees held on to the branches for dear life, but the fire that began consuming the forest was unforgiving. It devoured every one of them. The archers ran for their lives as the flames raced towards them, and the swordsmen found themselves surrounded, facing the menacing and salivating *Rakshashas* who were strong enough to break their ranks.

In less than half an hour, peace was restored in the clearing. The *Rakshashas* erupted into celebration after the ordeal was over. Fresh *soma* filled their glasses to the brim. Kicked, flung high into the air, ripped apart; the burnt body parts of Surya's soldiers became the entertainment for the night, though a few of the *Rakshashas* were wise enough to pick up the juiciest parts to satiate their appetite.

***

For the next few hours, Ram walked in silence. The sun's rays had grown kinder and the countryside was coming back to life. People who had been dreading the hot sun in the afternoon were now out on the streets and resumed their chores - fetching water from the nearby stream, jostling each other in the markets and selling their wares, elders pouring into the *chaupals* while the children played.

Suketu's house was built at the end of the village. Surrounded by large barren tracts of land on all sides brought about by the drought, it stood like an oasis in the desert. It was a multi-storied burnt, brick structure, guarded by three lines of precariously tied bamboo shafts acting as a boundary for his abode. The whole house was painted a deep shade of red ochre. 'Doing quite well in his life,' Ram thought looking at the house. A long dual line of guards was guarding its entrance. Since the house was surrounded by land without even a single blade of grass on its surface, guerrilla tactics were out of the window. Launching a direct onslaught against the men, who had already been alerted by Ram's presence, was the only way to reach Suketu. Holding his axe firmly, Ram increased his pace. The long journey had made him impatient. He wanted to be done with the job at hand.

From a distance, the guards saw a short, bare-bodied, bearded man waving a sharp hatchet and charging towards them. They remained idle for a few moments, trying to make sense of it. The Brahmin, an assumption based on his appearance, had a recognizable face. The many scars on his well-built physique told stories of the numerous adventures he had undertaken in his lifetime. Seeing the resolve on his face, the guards knew he wouldn't be subdued easily. They braced themselves to do what Suketu had been paying them for; protecting him from harm.

"Stop!" the man in front bellowed, unsheathing his sword menacingly.

The command had no effect on Ram's pace. The men warned him several times, brandishing their swords to no avail. Their enemy had covered a significant distance in the short time, and was now too close for comfort. The guard in front, who seemed to be in command of the unit, ordered his fellowmen to attack. Two men at the back started firing arrows in quick succession, but the enemy seemed to be an expert with his battleaxe. The arrows which were aimed at his heart were unable to break his run as he kept snipping the approaching darts mid-air using his axe. The arrows fell without incurring even a scratch on the sage's body. Two of the swordsmen ran towards Ram. However, before the group had time to brace themselves, they were struck down, bleeding profusely; their bodies mutilated. The men at the end of the row readied themselves to shoot another set of arrows as four heavily built men moved towards Ram.

Ram slid. His cleaver caught the first one on the groin. The man at his side slashed using his entire strength, but before his sword could touch him, Ram caught hold of his wrist. Pulling out his axe from the man's thighs, he ripped open the stomach of his opponent letting his guts spill. The next one in line ran towards the unstoppable sage. Another slash; another man cut open. Ram saw the arrows leaving the bows of his enemies. In no time, the whirlwind of a Brahmin had caught hold of the man standing before him and used him as a cover. His short stature was completely shielded by the burly man. Ram carried the man, now dead, for a distance, before taking a clear aim at one of the bowmen and flung his axe.

By that time, the men left standing had understood that Ram was a messenger of death for them. But owing to their duty, they kept fighting and lost their lives to his might. In no time, all, but one, laid on the ground either dead, or waiting for their painful demise. The man left standing started mumbling his final prayers directed towards the almighty, asking for forgiveness for all his sins. Ram reached the end of the row and held the only survivor, who was the bowman of the group, by his collar. Giving him a cold stare, he asked, "Where is Suketu?"

"Who are you? For what fault of ours have you killed so many?" the man wailed, struggling to free himself.

"Like my *Guru*, the endless, formless, timeless Shiva, I am everywhere and inside everyone. I am the eternal, the undead. I have lived in every age, and will be present in the future. I am the fire that consumes everything in its path. I am the maddening rage that blinds the senses. I am Ram, Parshuram," the Brahmin declared with a taut expression.

The man who was gasping for breath, pressed his palms together in respect and pointed towards the house. He closed his eyes and asked for forgiveness in a feeble voice. Taking the sharp end of an arrow that had fallen on the ground from the man's quiver, Ram slashed his throat. He placed the body, still struggling to breathe, gently on the ground and went inside the house.

Ram entered the front hall of the house. It was a big, almost empty area supported by pillars. He saw a man, almost white with fear, sitting on the floor in a corner, trying not to be seen from the outside. He was trembling violently, having watched the Brahmin's antics through the window and dreading his predicament. And now, as the same Brahmin stood before him with his bloodied axe and a face contorted with indignation, he wet himself; whatever warmth was left in his body escaped him.

"Did you kill those villagers for not paying the rent?" Ram roared.

Suketu ran towards the Brahmin and laid himself on his feet. "Forgive me, I have made a terrible mistake," he cried, trying to push a few words out from his choked throat.

Ram stared at him with cold, unforgiving eyes. Raising his right hand above his head, he gave his axe a ferocious swing. The axe struck Suketu's forehead and his brain popped out. Giving one last angry look to the corpse, Ram searched the house for other survivors. But the house seemed to be empty. Once satisfied, he exited the house through its back door. He was covered in the enemy's blood from head to toe. At one corner of the house's boundary, he found a freshwater well. Ram pulled up a bucket of water and washed his axe calmly. His task was over quicker than he had anticipated. Satisfied that the metallic sheen was restored, he took a quick bath before walking away from the scene of the rampage.

The sun had set, and the nervous energy that had been flowing through Ram since morning was subdued. The cold-water bath had given him a much-needed respite from the heat. He treaded slowly towards his home, enjoying the gentle wind caressing his wet cheeks. One of the temples dedicated to Lord Surya, Ram's erstwhile student, was quite nearby. Ram decided to pay a visit, in memory of his favourite student.

Taking a small detour, he reached the small decrypt temple which resembled the numerous ones scattered across the countryside. It was a small structure erected using dried mud, with a few miniature drawings on its walls. Though it was no taller than Ram, it was barely wide enough to house a small idol of the deity inside. The idol itself was fashioned using mud; its features not clearly defined. A small silver polished bow hanging from the idol's shoulder seemed to indicate it was the image of Lord Surya Shrestha. Ram saw the face of the deity glowing under the light of a few burning incense sticks and candles. People paid their respects to the deity by placing a few offerings at the entrance of the temple.

'Surya seems to be quite popular,' Ram mused, looking at the number of offerings. The village seemed to have retired for the night. Except for an old village woman who was sitting on the floor near the temple, the whole area was deserted. With her eyes closed, she was muttering a *bhajan* under her breath. At frequent intervals, she was offering wild berries to the deity from a sack in front of her. Ram watched her in silence for a while, praying for Surya's soul. Though he couldn't recognise a lot of the *bhajan's* words she was singing, it seemed to be written in praise of Surya's valour and righteousness. The woman continued her humming for the next few minutes. Once the sack was empty, Ram realized it was time for her to head back home. He too decided to resume his journey towards his *ashram*. But, to his surprise, he saw the old lady remove her gold nose ring and place it as an offering.

'Must be a huge occasion that called for it,' Ram thought, 'A great weight must have been removed from her chest.'

As the woman stood up to leave, Ram inquired politely, "Auspicious day today, mother?"

Taking her walking stick, the woman prepared herself for the journey on foot towards her home. Without looking at him, she replied, "Tadka died today." Her voice trembled as she uttered those words. Ram could see tears welling up in her eyes. It seemed she, too, had lost someone close to her to the *Rakshashi*.

"Who killed her?" Ram asked in a surprised voice.

"Ram and Lakshman," the village woman replied.

Ram stood dumbfounded for a few moments. He had met many brave men in his life; men who could put a formidable front against *devas,* and Surya Shrestha was the bravest among them. The one who had killed Tadka was no ordinary human being. Someone had thrown a direct challenge to Ravan. The time had come to make amends for his past.

<u>SAMVAD</u>

"Have you heard about *samudra manthan*?" the master asked. Jamdagni had forgotten to latch the door. It had been snowing since evening. The whiteness outside shined brilliantly under the moonlight. Covered by a couple of blankets, he laid next to his teacher. Shiva lay on his side facing Jamdagni, his body straight, with his blanket kept neatly folded near his feet. Jamdagni nodded in affirmation. The churning of the ocean had been mentioned in most of the books that he had read. He tried to recall the story. "Both the *Devas* and the *Asuras* participated together in the churning of the Kshirsagar - the ocean of milk. Mount Mandaar balanced on the back of Kashyap, the tortoise, which is considered an avatar of Vishnu, was used as the churning rod. Vasuki, the serpent which adorns Mahadev's neck, was curled around the mountain and acted as a rope. The Gods and the *Asuras* churned the ocean by pulling Vasuki at its ends." Jamdagni wondered about the whereabouts of Vasuki. He had been living with his master for so long, and yet, Vasuki remained elusive.

"And," the master prodded him to continue.

"The churning produced multiple objects, both good and evil in nature," Jamdagni resumed, "First came halahal, a poison deadly enough to wipe out the whole of mankind. It was only through Mahadev's intervention that such a catastrophe was prevented. The God of the Gods drank the deadly concoction. Among other things came out Chandra, the moon, Lakshmi, the Goddess of wealth and consort of Vishnu, Varuni, Sharanga, Kamdhenu, Parijat flower and *Nidra*. Finally, Amrut, the elixir of youth and eternity appeared, which was won over by the *Devas*."

Jamdagni observed his teacher closely. The blue tinge on his neck looked more intense than usual. Was it his imagination or the effect of the cold weather?

"That is a story for children," the master responded, "Never forget the philosophy behind it."

"The Kshirsagar is our mind which is churned constantly by good and evil thoughts; the Gods and the *Asuras*. The goal is to achieve *moksha*, freedom from all our desires; the Amrut. But before a man reaches *moksha*, he faces innumerable distractions, each one just as difficult to conquer. *Maya* projects confusing images and visions which try to dither a man from his path to salvation.

The first obstacle is halahal which represents pain and suffering; an integral part of human life. Man suffers because of his vices. *Maya* tries to amplify those vices, and keeps a man burdened by his ego. The vices are Chandra and the *Apsaras*, the celestial nymphs, which personify our attachment to physical beauty. Kaustubha, the divine jewel, Kamdhenu and Lakshmi constitute our attachment to wealth and prosperity. The irritable Varuni, the consort of the wind God, Varuna, stands for jealousy, *Nidra* for sloth, and Sharanga, the bow given to the *Asuras*, represents pride. Kalpavriksha, the wish-fulfilling divine tree and Parijat tree which blossoms for eternity exemplify our desire for youthfulness and eternal life.

A man who can conquer his vices like vanity, greed, pride, jealousy, anger, sloth, etc., ultimately attains *moksha* or salvation."

The story had a far deeper meaning than what Jamdagni expected. 'It would have been more suitable if it was narrated during the day,' thought the sleepy-headed Jamdagni. He was feeling cold. He walked towards the door and closed it. Coiling under his blanket, he felt *Nidra* enveloping him from all sides and gave into it.

RAVAN

He saw his brothers sitting at the north gate leading to the palace. The gate remained open till late in the evening, and commoners were allowed to enter freely. The road leading to it had been widened recently. From east to west, on a newly levelled, unwinding clearing, it allowed for at least twenty bullock carts to move alongside each other. A golden-hued, wooden framework rose majestically towards the sky. It was visible from at least one kilometre away. From a distance, it looked like a plain, heavy piece of shiny metal, planted solidly into the ground, but as you approached closer, the figures of *Yakshas*, *Rakshashas*, and *Nagas* etched intricately on the gate became clear. Gates with similar designs were erected on all four corners leading to the palace. He tried to remember who had worked on building it, but it seemed to be a distant memory. His brothers were seated on the stairs built on one side of the gate. It led to where the soldiers stood guard on top. A small group of uniformed army men surrounded them. They were listening intently to what the brothers were saying.

His two brothers were the monoliths on which the palace of Lanka stood; Vibhishan and Kumbhkarn, just towards their subjects, brave against their enemies, and loyal to their friends; the kind you would want on your side. While Vibhishan bore a grave demeanour and a slight reticence, Kumbhkarn was full of mirth and wit - people around him never had a bout of bad mood.

"Stay together and look out for each other," Kaikesi, his mother, used to say, "You have no one else in the world."

Today, Ravan understood the full meaning behind his mother's words. It seemed he had spent a lifetime building Lanka. Its foundations had been anointed with the blood and sweat of his near and dear ones. One day at a time, one brick at a time, the palace of Lanka had evolved into being. But it was only that day he realised that all his hard work had been in vain. Chandrahaas, the sword bearing the smile of a new moon, seemed to mock him. The sword had accompanied him multiple times on the battlefield to protect the throne of Lanka. But today, the same throne had betrayed him and his people. His half-brother Kuber, the ruler of Lanka, had turned against them. Casting off the troubling thoughts, Ravan returned his gaze towards the gates. His brothers had left their post and were nowhere to be seen. The subjects of Lanka were pouring into the fort's premises. He saw a woman, an emancipated soul, entering the gate with two skeletal figures tagging along next to her. 'Must be her children,' Ravan thought. The thin, reed-like figure of the mother looked ironic in front of the gold foliaged gate. Ravan felt his golden headgear tighten on his crown. The golden throne of Lanka and his *Yaksha* brother decked in gold from head to toe seemed to be ridiculing her existence. His grip on the Chandrahaas tightened. Lanka needed to be freed from the clutches of its king.

***

Kuber, a handsome man in his youth, who had been full of promise, had turned unkempt, bald and paunchy with age. Ravan had tried to retain his earlier image in his mind. When they were younger, girls from the neighbourhood would try finding excuses to visit his father's house.

"People scoff at our father's claim that the two of us have the same blood flowing through our veins. I need to distance myself from you; I shall start spending more time with Kumbhkarn," said Ravan in mock indignation. The brothers used to roam around their village.

Ravan had just caught a girl exchanging furtive glances with his *Yaksha* brother.

"All these muscles for nothing," Kuber laughed, feeling Ravan's biceps.

In contrast to the lean and toned body of Kuber, Ravan was a storehouse of pulsating muscles. From a distance, he looked no less than a boulder obstructing one's path.

"You need to practice more. Heera is about to retire," his father, Vishrava, would comment in jest looking at Ravan. Heera was the name of his father's bull which used to plough the fields.

Sage Vishrava was the master of a modest household who led a simple life with his two wives – Ilavida, mother of Kuber, and Kaikesi, mother of Ravan. Quite early in their lives, both the brothers had decided not to settle for the austerity their parents practiced. They were courageous and ambitious, and not afraid to take risks.

They lived in a small village in Indraprastha, an autonomous region under the kingdom of Hastinapur, west of Ayodhya. The brothers knew a day would come when they would have to leave their homeland to carve out their destinies. As a child, along with his elder brother, Ravan used to travel to distant lands. From freezing mountains, to the hottest deserts, to the deepest seas - there was no place on the map of the *Bharatvarsh* which the brothers hadn't experienced.

'Our land never ceases to amaze. It is the birthmother of all the ideas that have ever existed. It might be the birthmother of human consciousness,' was Ravan's constant response whenever he was asked to describe his travels.

It was during that period that the desire to move away from their homeland had become indelibly strong in the hearts of the brothers. Their experiences showed them how much the world had to offer, which was not possible to achieve while they lived in their remote village. Though Kuber and Ravan were unsure of what were they looking for, nevertheless, they continued their search.

Wherever they travelled to, the brothers drew attention to themselves. Kuber was extraordinarily handsome, while Ravan impressed people with his weapon-wielding skills. And if that was not enough, he surprised them by participating in philosophical arguments with even the most esteemed sages.

"Who taught you this?" Kuber shouted when he saw Ravan teaching sword fighting to children much older than him. The brothers had been visiting the kingdom of Kaikeya. Every morning, Ravan went to practice by the seashore. Within a few days, he had managed to gather a coterie who quickly grew fond of him. The group, along with Ravan, kept practicing at the shore whilst enjoying the cool morning breeze. It was time for the brothers to continue their journey. On their last day in Kaikeya, Ravan decided to teach a group of young boys a trick or two. Since he had already impressed them by showing them how to climb atop a galloping horse, at the moment, he was indulged in a fight against imaginary targets. Wielding swords in each hand, he was running at full speed while holding the horse's reins between his teeth.

"I am the favourite child of Brahma. I have known this since birth," Ravan bellowed, without breaking his pace and letting the reins fall from his grip.

***

It was one of the coldest winters that enveloped the whole country. By late evening, people retired indoors to curl under their blankets. It was past midnight when Kuber saw Ravan reading under the dim light of a torch, which hung in a corner of the room. The book in front of him contained pictorial explanations of various battle formations. Ravan had an unsatiated appetite for all kinds of books. Wherever he went, Ravan carried a big pile of books with him. That pile was replaced by another when he returned to his father's abode.

"I will be the most knowledgeable sage *Bharatvarsh* has ever seen." Ravan's teeth gleamed through the darkness that surrounded him.

Kuber laughed, "That might be true someday. Though, I am afraid whatever knowledge you gain is only feeding your ego."

"Deeper knowledge is not possible without being egoistic," Ravan said thoughtfully, "All major travails and adventures are the result of man's refusal to be tied down."

Kuber mulled over Ravan's words. Though he was feeling sleepy, his brother's talk sounded interesting. "It would be difficult to find someone so full of himself as we are," he remarked.

Ravan smiled, "It is only I who can surpass you at being an ass."

"You surpass me by leagues. You use long-winded sentences and circular arguments to prove your point. You even talk about being egoistic, as if it were a virtue," Kuber laughed.

"It is a great virtue," Ravan tried to choose his words, "Knowledge has always been quite an individualistic enterprise. Most of what we know today has already existed. It depends on the seeker of knowledge, and his willingness to push himself to his limits to discover it. A true seeker invests hours, days, and months in search of the unknown. Sometimes, he is unsure of what he would find at the end, or how the world would react to his pursuit, but he persists. And to persist against all odds, he needs an ego; a large, inflated ego; one which can devour everything around him; which makes everything look paltry before his objective. The ego drives him to sacrifice his mundane life, to follow new, uncharted territory; to sacrifice his family and friends to reach a pedestal which is quite difficult to reach. One has to be very selfish to gain true knowledge."

"And once you gain true knowledge, your ego melts," Kuber's interest was piqued.

Ravan smiled knowingly, "A seeker walks an egoistic journey of self-destruction. Ego pushes one to destroy itself. Once you reach the farthest point of knowledge, everything becomes quite insignificant in front of it; even your ego."

***

Kuber decided to leave Ravan to go alone on his journey. He too was looking to pave his own path to greatness. Being the eldest among his brothers, Kuber had seen how his poor parents had struggled with the birth of his siblings. Vishrava had wanted a girl, but the beautiful Surpanakha had made him wait in earnest for her arrival. She came into the world only after the birth of her three older brothers.

Established around Kuber's birth, the *ashram* run by Vishrava was the only source of income, but it slowly dwindled in strength over time. Bisrakh, the village where sage Vishrava resided, was peaceful. People from all over Hastinapur sent their children to this quaint place to study in solitude. However, in a decade since then, more *ashrams* were opened in the vicinity, and they were headed by reputed priests. Sage Vishrava tried with great difficulty to protect himself from the competition, but the young, energetic sages instituted novel and innovative ways of learning. In addition to that, Kuber's father took frequent recesses to look after his wife who had grown weaker with each birth. This made the students look for other teachers who employed more regularity with their classes. With time, the *ashram's* ill-repute of not completing its sessions on time got etched onto people's minds.

At a very young age, when his father's *ashram* was shut down, the responsibility to provide for the family fell on Kuber's shoulders. Every new life in the household meant an increase in the family's expenses, and nothing came cheap in Indraprastha. Every morning, Kuber toiled for long hours in the family's farm, and later went to the local market to sell small wares and dried wood. Taking whatever small chores the world threw at him, he tried to remain faithful to the needs of his family.

The importance of wealth, or the utter lack of it, was understood by Kuber when Ravan was born. It was the beginning of Kaikesi's illness from which she never truly recovered. Throughout her pregnancy, she suffered from severe, persistent nausea and vomiting. She grew pale, the colour fading from her cheeks, and lost weight at a rapid pace.

"That demon is playing havoc with my body," she cursed the unborn child, while Vishrava tried to console her.

It was during the fifth month of her pregnancy when she fainted three times in a single day. That day, Vishrava stopped teaching whatever students were left and sent them back to their homes. Along with Ilavida, he busied himself with looking after Kaikesi.

Ilavida tried to discourage her husband and coaxed him into resuming his classes, but Vishrava remained adamant. "She needs all the support we can muster." Every penny of Vishrava's savings was spent on buying medicines and supplements for Kaikesi, and it was Kuber's daily earnings which provided some support to the family.

After a few months, Kaikesi gave birth to a baby boy who wouldn't stop bawling. Ravan's birth had rendered her weak. The child, underweight and undernourished, lay beside his mother, crying at the top of his voice.

"Let us name him Ravan, the one with a thunderous roar," Kaikesi replied with a tired smile.

"He would remain a Ravan till he gets his share of feed. The child needs milk to survive," Vishrava said, looking worriedly at Kuber.

The money Kuber was earning was not enough to even provide staple grains for the whole household. It had been many weeks since his house had seen any milk. He stood dumbstruck before his father, searching his mind for a solution.

"No need to worry. I will talk to Daman tomorrow," Vishrava consoled him, placing the child back into his cradle. Daman was a rich dairy farmer who lived nearby. Kuber crossed his house every day on his way to the village market. He had seen his employees trying to sell the milk products in the market.

Many years ago, sage Vishrava had found a friend in Daman. At that time, Daman was a small-time fruit and vegetable vendor. He regularly supplied produce to the sage's *ashram*. Teeming with students, Vishrava's *ashram* had taken a significant amount of his produce. In the evenings, Daman would sit on the staircase leading to the raised platform where Vishrava took his classes. He would listen intently to his discourses with his students.

With the meagre savings he had at the time, Daman was able to buy a small piece of land in the village. Then, he tried his luck at opening a dairy farm. He was already taking care of the buffalos at the sage's *ashram*. It proved to be a profitable venture for him. Daman's cattle multiplied and he was able to bring in a lot of farmland. During those years, Vishrava's earnings from his *ashram* had steadily dwindled. While they both remained respectful of each other, Daman frequented his place less as time passed. He had other avenues to profiteer, which took a significant amount of his time. It was only then, after so many years had passed that sage Vishrava decided to visit Daman's farm. For a long time, their communication had been limited to greeting each other whenever their paths crossed in the village.

In the evening, Vishrava went to visit Daman, who was busy milking the cows. Even though he had many employees to take care of the cattle, he enjoyed working alongside them.

"It is an honour to see you at my abode." Daman washed his hands, seeing the sage entering with his son.

Vishrava enquired about his family and his business. He slightly hesitated before stating his real purpose. He could already feel a lump forming in his throat. He kept looking at Kuber, who stood by his side flinching impatiently. Sensing his reservation, Daman had to ask, "Tell me, Vishrava, what is troubling your mind?"

"Kaikesi has just given birth to a baby boy." Daman nodded. He had already congratulated the father when he'd met him earlier at the local market. "The child needs nourishment and his mother is too weak to provide it. It would be great if you can supply us with a few *chhataanks* of milk every day."

Daman gave a hearty laugh. "What makes you so nervous about asking for it? This is what I look forward to - new customers. I would be glad to fulfil your requirements."

But Vishrava wasn't finished with his request. "It would be great if you can provide it for free - for the time being. Consider it as a debt to me. I don't have any money to pay you right now." The shame of indebtedness was imprinted on Vishrava's forehead. His voice started cracking.

Daman thought for a moment, "When can you return the money? Do you have any plans to restart your *ashram*?"

The sage could not lie. He knew it would be difficult for him to repay the money. "I will try my best to pay you as soon as possible."

Daman was a witness to Vishrava's dwindling financial condition. He sighed deeply. "The debt will keep increasing, Vishrava. Today, you stand before me asking for milk. But your needs won't end here. You will keep asking for debt from others."

Vishrava stood shamefaced, unable to give a convincing solution. "You doubt my intentions?"

"Who am I to doubt sage Vishrava's intentions?" said Daman, his words dripping with sarcasm, "But I am unable to see how you will repay it."

Kuber stood listening to the conversation. He saw his father bring his palms together in a respectful *namaskar* and bow his head, looking meekly at Daman. Vishrava's efforts to prevent his voice from choking had turned his face red.

"Help a poor man's son, Daman. I will remain indebted to you for life," pleaded Vishrava.

Daman looked sympathetically towards the sage. "That is what I fear, Vishrava. I don't need your indebtedness. I need money in return for my goods."

"At least do it for the sake of an old friendship?" Kuber spoke at last, his face flushed.

Daman replied in a polite voice, "Prove your worth as a good son to your father. He needs your support now, more than ever."

Before Kuber could speak further, Vishrava asked for Daman's leave.

"You can take some for today," Daman called from behind, pointing towards a bucketful of milk. But Vishrava pretended he hadn't heard him and walked back towards his *ashram*. On their way back, Kuber found it difficult to meet his father's eyes.

"Being humiliated by others drives a stake through one's heart. But seeing the shame written all over your parents' face can shatter it into a million pieces," Kuber had once told Ravan while recalling the incident.

Every evening, while returning from the market, Kuber saw Daman busy milking the cows. And every day when he returned home, he came to the worried faces of his parents; the child in their lap crying inconsolably.

"Just a little more time, son," said Ilavida, holding the child close to her chest, "The hunger will subdue your whimpers in a few days." Kuber's mother had big, round tears in her eyes.

"What kind of a father am I? His bawls hurt my conscience more than my ears," Vishrava confided in Kuber one day.

That very night, it was much colder than usual. Kuber, along with his parents, was unable to sleep. Ravan seemed to have turned deaf to the pleas of his elders. He decided to put his foot down, and no amount of coaxing could make him sleep. Kaikesi's breasts were dry as ever. She was too weak and cold to hold Ravan close to her. It was Ilavida who kept rocking him throughout the night while she remained sleep-deprived, but it seemed the child had decided to fight for his survival. Even after being hungry for so many days, the shrillness of his cry revealed his zeal to live. Kuber watched the whole scene in silence, shamefaced at being unable to help his family.

A day later, while returning from the market, Kuber approached a small goat shed constructed on Daman's land. It was situated a bit further away from where he kept his cows. Taking a small flask hidden under his clothes, Kuber started milking a couple of goats. The goats remained unperturbed by his presence, making the task easy for him. Within no time, he was back on the streets with the flask filled to the brim with warm milk, hanging across his chest.

Back home, Kuber hid the container from the eyes of his parents. It was only when everyone went to sleep that he tiptoed towards Ravan's cradle. The raspy breathing of the child could be heard from a distance. Taking a small cotton ball, Kuber wetted it with milk to feed Ravan. The child greedily sucked at it. The hunger was evident in his eyes. He kept feeding Ravan until the container was nearly half-empty.

"This is enough for the day. Don't you turn sick on me," Kuber whispered before corking the flask. He placed Ravan gently back on his cot, and took his place beside his parents, pretending to be asleep.

It was Vishrava who first awoke in the morning. He looked outside the window, and cursed himself when he saw the sun shining in all its brilliant glory. It was the first night since Ravan's birth that he had been able to sleep soundly, and that was his cause for worry.

'The child didn't even whimper last night,' he thought. Vishrava rushed towards Ravan's cradle, only to find him sound asleep with a gentle smile playing on his face. Compared to the previous day, his skin seemed to have gained some colour. The edge in his rasping seemed to have weaned off, too.

"He seems to recognise you. His smile widens whenever he sees you," Ilavida remarked as Kuber took Ravan in his lap.

"I am taking him outside. I think he needs some fresh air," said Kuber before leaving the room with Ravan. On reaching a short distance away from home, he took the flask out and fed Ravan again.

"Growing heavy already," Kuber remarked, feeling Ravan's weight. The child was lapping up the milk happily.

It soon became a habit. Every couple of days, Kuber would visit Daman's goat shed surreptitiously. Within a few minutes, he was out of the premises and hopping home with the flask full of milk. Once home, he looked for opportunities to find Ravan alone.

In those few weeks, Kaikesi almost recovered from her bout of illness, and the child who had been struggling to survive a month ago turned chubbier and was full of life. His wails were a thing of the past. To their parents' relief, his general disposition turned pleasant, and it was a lot easier to make him laugh.

"He is gaining weight. It is nothing short of a miracle to see him responding so well to the medicine." Ilavida had prepared a concoction using the herbs that grew around the *ashram.* She was under the impression that it was her medicine which had cured Ravan's ailment.

"All great things in life extract a heavy price from you," she used to say, while administering the bitter medicine to Ravan as the child grimaced.

The routine continued until one afternoon, Vishrava saw Kuber feeding Ravan; the flask containing milk was kept open. Like every other day, Kuber had waited until his parents had finished their lunch, and gone for a siesta. He then took Ravan outside the house to the raised platform where Vishrava used to administer classes for his students. A thirst induced by the hot afternoon sun had caused Vishrava to wake. It was only then that he realised the reason behind Ravan's improving health. Without thinking twice, he slapped Kuber, his palm meeting squarely across Kuber's cheek.

"Don't ruin the name of your family. It doesn't suit a sage's son to steal," Vishrava said angrily.

"It also doesn't suit a sage's son to go hungry," Kuber replied, throwing away the cotton ball and leaving the child with his father. It had been so many days since Ravan resumed bawling, on seeing himself unceremoniously transferred back into his father's arms.

But Kuber's humiliation didn't end here. In the evening, Vishrava took him to Daman, and in a polite tone explained his son's doing, asking for forgiveness.

"I think you didn't hear me when I refused to provide milk for free that day," Daman said, on hearing the incident. "Do you start stealing someone's property if he refuses to give you alms? Is this what Brahmin children do?"

Kuber felt his ears burn. He waited for Daman's tirade to end.

"During my early days here, your father had been kind to me. I have seen him exchange wise words with his students. But it seems he spared none for his sons," Daman said caustically. It was Vishrava's turn to feel the burn while Kuber raised his bloodshot eyes.

"You refuse to part with an ounce of milk for a dying child, fathered by the man you call your friend," Kuber replied as tears flowed freely from his eyes. "How else could I save my brother? What other options did I have apart from stealing?"

"If you dare raise your voice again, I will take you by the collar and hand you over to the local chief," Daman roared. "We always have options. But we are afraid to exercise it and try to find an easy way out. You should have tried to earn it. That is what I did," Daman said pointing to himself, "When your father was busy losing students, I used to straighten my back and leave to sell my goods every day. Be it cold chilly mornings or hot afternoons, for fifteen years I have toiled without fail and this is what I did."

Daman paused to reminisce about his old days. His voice turned soft, "I too have had my share of bad days, but I've never duped anyone. Earn your place in this world, son. You won't be able to steal it, and no one would be kind enough to yield it to you."

While returning home, Kuber looked towards his father. It was the first time he had realised it; the reason behind the constant sadness he saw in his eyes. They reflected his defeat at the hands of fate.

Ravan was sleeping in Ilavida's arms when Kuber entered, along with Vishrava. He took Ravan in his lap and whispered, "We will earn it."

***

"Why has the *rishi* refused to allow us into his *ashram*?" Ravan asked his mother. They had just returned from a sage's place. Vishrava wanted to admit his three younger sons to the same *ashram* where Kuber had pursued his studies.

"Don't worry. I shall be your teacher," Vishrava said, before leaving the room in a huff. "From now on, Kuber too doesn't need to go to that place," he added.

"Why was Kuber selected when we were left out?" Ravan questioned, returning his attention to his mother.

"What do you think might be the reason?" Kaikesi snapped. She knew Ravan was wise enough to know the answer.

Ravan thought for a while. A single word escaped his lips, "*Rakshasha.*"

"That is your armour. Wear it with pride," Kaikesi softened, "Vishrava is a kind man. I can understand how difficult it must have been for him to accept me as his wife. It caused a huge dent to his reputation. Ever since I was your age, I envied every one of those highborn. Everything came so easy to them while we needed to prove ourselves at each stage. It was only because of your father that you were even able to see the inside of another *ashram*. Try visiting one without using his name."

This was not the first time that Ravan's *Rakshasha* identity had become evident. Every time such incidents happened; his insides churned. A sense of guilt descended into his heart for no fault of his own. He felt caged, unable to do what he wanted because of something that could not be erased.

"I wanted to study with the other children," Ravan said. "Even Saundarya got admitted to the same *ashram*." Saundarya was the son of a local farmer who lived in the neighbourhood. He used to visit Vishrava's *ashram* almost every evening to play with the other children.

Ravan looked towards his mother. Her eyes were bereft of any pity for his plight. Kaikesi was a proud *Rakshashi*. She tried to gauge Ravan's emotions. Her son looked uneasy by Saundarya's admittance.

"Has your pride been bruised enough?" she probed Ravan. Looking towards her other sons, she said, "Now, we all know what happened. The question we need to ask ourselves is how, despite the circumstances, we will not allow ourselves to fall behind in life."

Ravan didn't have a definite answer for it. His brothers too looked equally lost. Their silence perturbed Kaikesi. She hadn't expected it from her sons; at least, not from her oldest one. She looked sharply towards Ravan, "Teach yourself everything that can be taught. And never forget your brothers in your quest. From now on, don't let this world come between you and your destiny."

That evening, Saundarya arrived at Vishrava's *ashram* to play with the other children. He knew he wouldn't find Ravan in a good mood. Patting his back, he said in a gentle voice, "No matter what happens, I will always have your back. You can count on me."

Ravan smiled. "Ask your teacher to admit me into his *ashram*."

Saundarya hesitated for a moment. He answered with all sincerity, "I will teach you everything I learn there."

"That won't be needed," Ravan laughed, "I just need admission for my brothers and myself to that *ashram*."

Saundarya found it difficult to meet Ravan's eyes, "You know how it is, Ravan. It has been that way for centuries."

"And will it remain that way for centuries?" Ravan questioned, "Go home, Saundarya. It is not suitable for you to spend time with us."

'*Rakshasha*,' the word kept ringing in Ravan's ears the entire time. He could see how his fate was much better when compared to his brethren. The *Rakshashas* were not allowed inside the village. They lived at the boundaries, depending on alms from others, with no land to claim as their own. Despite being married to a Brahmin, Kaikesi and her sons had never been fully accepted by the villagers. No matter how hard Ravan tried, people never allowed his family to forget their origins.

"But you are a Brahmin too. The son of a well-reputed sage," Kuber reminded Ravan once.

Ravan laughed boisterously, "Have you asked any Brahmin that?"

"They would realise it someday. I mean, looking at the speed with which you devour texts, they will soon be aware of the insatiable *Rakshasha* appetite of this Brahmin," Kuber added laughing. He had seen Ravan continuously scan through his books, without any sleep for days.

Ravan looked towards Kuber with bloodshot eyes, "With their half-baked knowledge, they can open large *ashrams*. Some might even become high priests of renowned temples, while others become advisors to great kings. But no matter how much knowledge I gain, such doors would always remain closed to me."

"You should not be so hard on yourself, Ravan," Kuber comforted his younger brother. "People will remember you for your knowledge."

"I will make sure they remember," said Ravan, "I will show them how the will of a *Rakshasha* shall surpass all ambitions. The collective experience our tribe has rendered us infallible. I will make the *Rakshasha* clan realise it."

Kuber walked in silence for a while before adding thoughtfully, "I just hope I never overstep your pride."

"You are a progeny of the *Yakshas*. It would be difficult to find someone as proud as you," Ravan sneered.

Kuber smiled wryly, "What is it that you want to prove to the world?"

"That I am an equal," said Ravan, "if not more."

Due to sage Vishrava's efforts, all his sons proved to be quite self-sufficient in learning. With the help of available resources, they supported each other in the theoretical as well as the practical concepts of a subject. In the beginning, Vishrava had been apprehensive about how his experiment with tutoring his sons would work. But Ravan's voracious appetite for knowledge and his constant prodding to keep pace with others helped ease his mind.

"It was a great white horse, almost twice my size. Its shiny mane swayed back and forth as the beast moved. On its back was a gold-plated saddle strapped to leather holsters, on which Sushena was seated. His face shone brilliantly in the afternoon sun. On his head was a silver crown with the word Bisrakh embossed in large letters. The smooth silk he wore flowed gently in the wind as the horse galloped. His shoes, made of snakeskin, caused people to avert their gaze as the sun reflected against its brilliant glare," Vibhishan paused to catch his breath.

Kaikesi stole glances at Ravan while Vibhishan spoke. He was describing the appearance of the village chief's son whom he'd seen that morning. He was leading a small contingent out of the village. It was only towards the end of Vibhishan's monologue that Ravan realised his mother's eyes were riveted towards him.

"What do you desire?" Kaikesi asked Ravan.

"Everything belongs to me," said Ravan.

"Why?" asked Kaikesi.

"He wants to be rich like him," Kuber said, looking meaningfully towards Ravan.

Ravan laughed. Money was the last thing on his mind.

"Because I deserve it more than them. They try to keep me bound by the circumstances of my birth. I will turn their world upside down," said Ravan, the *Rakshasha* pride bleeding from each word. "While we have to fight for every small privilege, everything comes easy to them."

Exactly a year after that day, Vibhishan, Kumbhkarn and Kuber were sitting at the entrance of their *ashram*. The monsoons had arrived, and it had rained heavily throughout the night. The coolness in the air was a respite from the unending bout of summer Bisrakh had been witnessing for a month. The gentle caress of the wind lulled the brothers to sleep. They raised their heads as the dull monotony surrounding them was broken by the gentle trot of a horse. They saw their brother riding atop the same great white horse Vibhishan had described many months before. The snakeskin shoe Ravan wore gleamed brilliantly in the light.

"Meet the new village chief," Ravan said dismounting from the horse. His brothers watched with their mouth open.

Ravan laughed placing the silver crown with Bisrakh embossed on Kuber's head, "It has just begun."

***

As children, the four brothers used to play a game where each of them assumed the title of king, and tried to defend their imaginary kingdoms. They would go on a treasure hunt and try to find items of 'value' from the jungles that surrounded them. Feathers of a bird found rarely, a white sandstone rendered smooth by the river, the broken fang of a snake; the value of the items brought was decided through mutual agreement. Using those items, they would be able to buy foot soldiers, cavalry, infantry or any combination of the three to protect their fort. They could also use them to strengthen their fort by surrounding it with a moat or placing archers on its parapet. The brothers could attack the fort of the others whenever they were convinced of their strength. If one was defeated, the other became the master of his remaining army. The game continued until there was a clear winner.

Not much time passed since their childhood games became real. The brothers found themselves embroiled in small battles with trying to protect their land and expanding their dominion. Through their enterprise, they were able to win a small region south of Dandaka *van*. They now had a regular army which answered to their command.

However, the call to their ambitions remained unanswered.

"We need to capture more forts," Kuber used to say, recalling the childhood game.

With the help of Ravan and his other brothers, Kuber wanted to expand his influence. Currently, they were the masters of a few villages. None of the brothers had any ideas on how to turn their small chiefdom into a kingdom of consequence. Their minds were bereft of any plans. It was only Ravan who understood Kuber's impatience to succeed. Later at night, when the brothers slept outside in the open, under the millions of stars winking at them, Ravan would look towards Kuber and say, "Do what you need to do, and I will always be with you."

Sage Vishrava's children were born in an era when the mainland was fraught with ambitious rulers and mighty generals. Each kingdom was competing against the other, vying for glory. Embroiled in numerous battles, *Bharatvarsh* was losing its brave sons at a rapid pace. Wherever the brothers looked, they found two giants pitted against each other.

"Kuber – a local chief and nothing more," a dry smile was playing on Kuber's face. The sea waves were splashing against the rocky shore which refused to yield. He sat with Ravan, looking at the vast expanse of water in front of them.

"The king of Kishkindha – Riksharaj was once a small-time chief of his tribe," Ravan said trying to assuage his brother's bruised ego.

"Don't forget how old he was when he was anointed king," Kuber said laughingly.

Ravan looked towards the horizon. The sun was about to set. It was getting difficult to pinpoint the bright blue of the large stone he wore on his right index finger. It garnered a blackish hue as the night approached.

"We can try to bring Venad under our influence," Ravan said looking towards the stone. Venad was a small kingdom bordering the land they ruled.

"The Cholas support its autonomous status," said Kuber, referring to one of the strongest kingdoms in the south, "If we dare touch Venad, within no time, we would become their vassals."

Ravan nodded. He chided himself for forgetting the influence of the Cholas.

"What makes them so strong?" Ravan asked, "The Cholas."

"Money," said Kuber, "It is the simplest fact. Power begets money and vice versa."

"We should look for money then," Ravan whispered, his jaws turning stiff.

"I could sense you turning green," Kuber laughed. Kuber was no stranger to Ravan's competitive spirit.

"I want to see your colours once we become rich," Ravan smiled. Both the brothers remained engrossed in their thoughts for a while.

"Where did you get this?" Kuber broke the silence. The stone on Ravan's finger caught his attention.

"Bought it from the local market in Venad," he said.

"When you went there for Subhalakshmi's *swayamvar*?" asked Kuber, to which Ravan nodded. Subhalakshmi was the princess of Venad who had gotten married the previous week. Ravan was invited to the occasion as the state's guest.

"I don't think it is mined there. They must be importing it from some other state," Kuber continued. He was enamoured by the impressive finish of the stone.

"Lapis Lazuli is its name. From what I know, large ships containing silk and other textiles are dispatched from Lothal, and they bring back gold and other jewels from far-off countries in the west. These stones are quite expensive as the ships take huge risks and cover a great distance to procure it. You want it?" Ravan asked smiling, seeing Kuber eyeing the stone.

"Venad produces the finest silk. I have seen their markets flooded with the produce," said Kuber ignoring the sarcasm hidden in Ravan's question. Each of Kuber's fingers was already decorated with precious stones. Diamond, ruby, gold; all shining brilliantly, even in the dull sunlight.

"Yes, but they are far from the best. The extremely good quality is exported to Lothal. It fetches a huge price in the foreign market," said Ravan. Lothal was a large city near the sea, embracing the western coast of *Bharatvarsh*. Since ancient times, it had been a popular trade centre. It served as an opening to interact with countries lying towards the west of the mainland. Ships laden with all kinds of goods left for far-off lands from the port of Lothal.

"How do they cover such large distances? It must wear out the sailors terribly," Kuber seemed curious to know more about the sea trade. It was good to have a scholar like Ravan by his side. He seemed to know everything.

"The journey is not completed in one stretch. There are many ports built along the way. After every ten *yojans* or so, these sailors halt to rest and repair their ships. The entire journey takes many months to complete," said Ravan.

"What about these kingdoms? Are they rich like Lothal?" asked Kuber excitedly, referring to the resting grounds of the sailors. His eyes glittered, imagining the wealth these kingdoms might hold.

"More than you can imagine. A lot has been written about these legendary cities. More people die in these cities because of greed rather than starvation. In case of medical emergencies, kings and emperors of our land go to these cities for treatment. Their roads are paved with gold and every household makes enough money to live without any worries," answered Ravan.

"Trade seems to be quite lucrative for them," Kuber pondered, his mind filled with ideas.

"Yes, trade, and moreover, their monopoly over it. Acting as the major trade point has helped them grow strong quickly. They impose hefty taxes on ships, and they protect their status with great vengeance. A few kings from neighbourhood kingdoms tried building ports in the past, but their efforts were thwarted vehemently. The current port cities are quick to cut down competitors who try duplicating their idea. And the money they had accumulated in the last few years helps them take care of it. Money begets power," Ravan smiled.

"One day when I become a great king, I will make you my foreign and trade policy minister," Kuber said laughing, before turning thoughtful, "Even kingdoms like Venad look towards Lothal for conducting such trade. Though, they are very close to the sea, down south."

"Why wouldn't they? These islands are full of uncouth people. It is a wasteland. They have lived in harmony with nature for ages. The laws of civilisation are lost on them," said Ravan.

"You are only talking about Lanka, Ravan. What about the lands further south?" said Kuber, his eyes narrowed while looking towards the horizon.

Ravan searched his memory. The texts he had read were too sparse when it came to descriptions about the southern neighbours of *Bharatvarsh*. It was only Lanka which he'd found scant mentions of, in certain places, as being a densely forested land filled with clans of *Rakshashas*.

"So much wealth might be hidden from our eyes, waiting to be discovered. It might be quite fruitful if we focus our energy on exploring these lands," Kuber said pointing towards the sea.

Ravan didn't harbour any doubts about Kuber's enterprising nature. He had spent quite a few years matching his will against Kuber's and found that they were not suited for the austere life of a Brahmin, like their father. But he was not too sure about the 'hidden wealth' Kuber kept talking about. They sat in silence for another hour, lost in their thoughts, before retiring for the day.

For the next few days, Ravan got busy with his daily schedule and almost forgot about the conversation he had had with Kuber about the southern kingdoms. It seemed Kuber's initial exuberance about the idea was consumed by reality. The hand of destiny was yet to deal its cards. At that time, Ravan didn't have the slightest inkling that he would be spending the next few years building an empire in Lanka. It was not long after when Kuber again raised the subject of Lanka.

"No one bothers with that speck of land," said Ravan, voicing his earlier concerns.

"And that is why we would be able to capture it without much opposition. If we rule Lanka, it will prove a gold mine for us," Kuber said excitedly, his eyes glistening with ambition. "We will bring civilisation to those people. The people residing there have no idea about its geographical advantage. Here," said Kuber referring to the mainland, "we can either fight until we are old, or die a miserable death in one such war. We will strike gold if we are able to capture Lanka. We will use its wealth to build our defences. Within a few years, we can govern the whole mainland from there."

From what Ravan knew about Lanka, it had no means to raise some substantial revenue for its ruler. No major agricultural activity or any other form of enterprise was practiced there. Its separation from the mainland by the sea made it quite difficult to govern. The other kingdoms in *Bharatvarsh* didn't see a tactical advantage in capturing it.

Kuber's conviction contradicted the strategy which had been followed for centuries - to leave the Lankans to their fate.

"I hope what we are planning has some value," Ravan said. The mention of the mainland's conquest had piqued Ravan's interest. He decided to follow Kuber's hunch.

"You leave that to me, brother," said Kuber, turning his determined gaze towards the shore, "You do what you are best at; winning battles."

Kuber's mother Ilavida was a *Yakshini*, a race known for their beauty, in contrast to the supposedly barbaric *Rakshasha* race from which Ravan was born. *Yakshas* were not known for hardships or fighting wars. These coarse ambitions suited the 'lesser' refined *Rakshashas*. *Yakshas* were known for their vanity and business acumen. For Kuber, Ravan might be one of the most competent military generals, but he wasn't fit to be a king; a role he espoused for himself.

The brothers didn't delay their expedition once they had made up their minds. For days, Ravan pored over the map of Lanka. He tried to gather as much information about the island as he could. Only a few people had had any contact with the teardrop-shaped island. There were a few *Rakshashas* within Ravan's ranks who had migrated to the mainland many years ago. Enlisting their help, Ravan noted down the names and strengths of different tribes who exercised their influence on different parts of Lanka. He wanted to land his small army in a sparsely populated region. He knew his soldiers would need some time to rest after the long journey.

To their advantage, the many tribes who inhabited the island had their own disparate culture, and occupied autonomous areas far from each other's influence. They had fought amongst each other for centuries which weakened their fraternal bonds. The modern ways of living were lost on them. They survived off the forest that surrounded them. Even their weapons, as per Ravan's knowledge, were built using forest wood.

After an arduous journey, the army led by Ravan landed at a desolate rocky sea beach in Lanka. It was not a large troop; the numbers were restricted to a few hundred, which included the cavalry. The soldiers needed time to acclimatize to the humid local weather. They decided to camp on the shore for a few days. Surrounded by thick equatorial jungles, it rained almost every afternoon on the beach. The jungles had enough fruits and shrubs to sustain a large army. It was unfamiliar territory for them. While Ravan and the others tried to research the place thoroughly, the fear of the unknown sometimes gripped their hearts at night; but not for long.

Within a week, Kuber asked them to get the perimeter secured. As the soldiers delved deep inside the thick forest, they encountered their first challenge. A group of several hundred men and women, armed with rudimentary bows, stood courageously, facing Ravan's army. The soldiers sat watching on horseback; their metal swords reflecting the beams of sunlight stubborn enough to cut across the thick canopy. The soldiers, befuddled by the motley group facing them, looked towards their commander for instructions.

"We are not here to harm you. Surrender and we will set you free," Ravan implored to the tribals.

But it seemed the words were lost on them. A woman with an unusually large head, short in stature, long-matted hair reaching the ground, and tattoos crisscrossing her body limped ahead of the group. Multiple necklaces made of different shiny stones jangled with her movements. Her sharp gaze revealed her murderous intent to Ravan as she began speaking ferociously in a dialect unknown to Kuber's soldiers.

Ravan called out to a translator accompanying his army; a Lankan local who had migrated to the mainland many years prior. "This forest belongs to me. I am the provider and the protector of its people. Return to your wretched land or I will make your soldiers burn as bright as the sun," the woman spoke.

Ravan and his army looked on with open amusement at the woman. Seeing them stand their ground without retreating, the woman started chanting a few mantras in a high-pitched voice. Taking the bow hanging on her shoulders in her hand, the ends of which were decorated with ivory, she pointed it towards the chief of Kuber's army. An arrow with a sharpened wooden tip, decked with birds' feathers at its end was loaded against the taut string.

The woman's voice grew shrill as Ravan saw the tribesmen lowering their weapons, and bowing their heads in deference. Ravan was surprised to see the feathers change colour every time the woman paused her incantations. The woman fired the dart towards Ravan, aiming for his skull. Ravan shifted his weight a bit and caught the arrow mid-flight.

"Enough of this sorcery. We don't want to harm you. Surrender at your will," he repeated, breaking the arrow and throwing it away in disdain. The tribals looked surprisingly towards their spellcaster.

The woman loaded another arrow and fired it in Ravan's direction, aiming for his chest. This time, Ravan didn't react. He let the arrow strike his metal armour and watched it fall to the ground. He pulled out his sword and pointed its sharp end towards the magician. The sword swung through the air and struck the woman's throat. With a loud thud, the woman fell flat on the ground. The soldiers saw the tribesmen looking wide-eyed in horror at the scene before them.

"Drop your weapons and yield," the plea in Ravan's voice was evident.

But the *Rakshasha's* tribe wanted to prove its mettle. "Protect your motherland," Ravan heard the collective cry of the enemy's ranks. The arrows came raining towards him. Like their chief, Kuber's army was well protected against such crude weapons. They galloped towards the tribesmen and started culling them swiftly. One followed the other, as the tribals fell, in their brave, yet foolish effort to protect their homeland. In no time, the area was cleared of the locals, with none left to pose any harm.

The trained soldiers of Kuber's army moved to other parts of the island. They didn't have any problems in seizing the Lankan lands. But not before the locals had displayed ample evidence of their *Rakshasha* descent by their imposing ferocity. Armed with pointed sticks, heavy stones, and wooden bows, they stood against the razor-sharp swords and heavy maces. Most of them chose to fight till the end. The war ended only when they had lost a significant number of their young men, leaving the old, destitute, and the children at the mercy of Ravan's forces. They spoke a different tongue which made it difficult for Ravan's generals to converse. They tried to persuade the tribes to stop resisting by using signs and symbols. But their efforts were wasted. The *Rakshasha* blood continued boiling and spilling over the shores of Lanka.

After a few such instances, strict instructions were issued to the soldiers. "Contain the bloodshed. They are our own," Ravan ordered. It was made clear that the life of the locals would only be taken if they posed a lethal danger to their army.

"The throne of Lanka is awash with the *Rakshasha's* blood," Ravan heard a soldier remark.

***

Within no time, Ravan and his army, under the leadership of Kuber, were able to bring most of the Lankan shores on the western side of the island under their control.

"You only need to win the coastal lands, the rest of it will buckle from inside," Kuber had strategized at the beginning of their campaign. Ravan wanted his army to circumscribe the island as the victories were obtained without much opposition, but Kuber was impatient to bring the next stage of their plan into action.

"Let us keep it aside for another day, Ravan. We will try to consolidate the territories we have won," he opinionated, looking at Ravan and Vibhishan.

Vibhishan looked at them quizzically, while Ravan nodded. There was not much to consolidate. The piece of land they had brought under their control was almost equal to what they ruled on the mainland; besides being thinly populated.

"We must push further. Within a few weeks, we will lose the element of surprise in our attacks," said Vibhishan in a worried tone, "the soldiers too are ready to fight."

"You seriously think we need to take our enemies by surprise to defeat them. Look at them," Kuber said pointing towards the makeshift prison of his camp, "Lanka is ours for the taking. We are the flag bearers of modern civilisation here."

The might of the small, yet trained army, that they possessed, was many times greater than the many tribes they had to conquer. But the restless warrior spirit of the youthful Vibhishan kept pushing him towards the battlefield.

"The inertia we have set would be lost," Vibhishan said, trying to raise the interest of his brothers.

Ravan smiled and patted his back, "There are more important things you need to take care of while I leave to explore other islands. You need to recruit more locals," he revealed their plan to Vibhishan, "Add numbers to our army. Train the Lankans with modern weapons so that they can be put to good use. They are *Rakshashas*. Courage flows in their veins. Learning to fight with modern weapons won't be too difficult for them. Let us also recruit a few of them for the administrative roles in our court. We are still a foreign force in Lanka. We need a few local faces among our ranks to validate our rule. Naked coercion won't take you too far. There needs to be a certain degree of acceptance of your rule among the masses."

"When do you plan to leave?" Vibhishan asked, "Kumbhkarn can accompany you on your journey."

"No, he is needed here," Ravan said looking at Kuber, "the ports at Lanka need to be designed large enough to anchor huge ships. Ask Kumbhkarn to start working on the plans as soon as possible. We have enough land to build a couple of them. I will be fine travelling alone."

Kuber embraced Ravan warmly, "Hope we find what we are looking for. It hasn't been explored to date. We will be creating history, my brother."

Within a few months, Ravan and his entourage returned to Lanka. Not too far was an archipelago called 'Suvarnbhoomi', the land of the gold. Along the way, they had found multiple inhabited islands rich in resources. While leaving for the unknown lands, Ravan had carried with him a few specimens of different items from the mainland like silk, cotton, sugarcane, and jewels. This created enough excitement among the locals. As the brothers had anticipated, the conquest of Lanka was going to be the catalyst in capturing the whole mainland. *Bharatvarsh*, one of the most prosperous lands of its times, was envied for its multiple trade relations with far-off lands. Till date, it was the western ports that had acted as the vistas to interact with the outside world. All the other kingdoms, landlocked or otherwise, would export their goods through these ports. This had made the western kingdoms richer by many leagues.

Kuber and Ravan, through their discovery and the conquest of Lanka, managed to change the existing dynamics. Building a port in Lanka opened another route hitherto unexplored. The discovery of Suvarn-bhoomi ignited a frenzy; the monopoly of which lay in the hands of the brothers. Once the trade potential with the archipelago was well established, they started charging a hefty fee for the use of Lankan harbours for trade.

"We need more ports," Vibhishan observed, seeing a large number of ships scampering for anchorage.

"Development can only happen in a peaceful environment. Let us keep our enemies at bay while we prosper." Kuber had already jotted down the areas near the sea where the new ports would be built. "Our monopoly should extend up till the Suvarnbhoomi. Lanka will serve as the main link between it and the *Bharatvarsh*."

While multiple players divided the revenue amongst themselves at the western line of trade, Kuber's plan was to monopolise the southern line.

"It would help if we lowered our fee in comparison to our counterparts in the west," Ravan complemented his brother's chain of thoughts.

With the revenue flowing in, the brothers directed their attention towards the other tribes left to conquer. The tribes controlling the seas were attacked and subjugated first. While the conquests provided fresh recruits for the army, the revenue generated through the port activities was used to modernise it and buy new weapons.

Seeing the wealth of the foreigners on their land multiply, few clans tried to emulate their ways. But they proved to be too late an entrant into the race. The sophisticated methods to construct a port were lost on them. Kuber had trained architects to build sturdy designs that could withstand rough weather. They also had a modern military which thwarted any attempt by the opposition to build a port pitted against their own. The whole enterprise to establish a functioning port proved quite costly to the tribes.

Ships from all over the *Bharatvarsh* had started pouring in, causing the Lankan treasury to overflow. The risk the brothers had undertaken had proved to be much more fruitful than they had imagined.

In a few months, Vibhishan returned with the news that the army had circumscribed the whole territory of Lanka. It had gained control of all the sea routes. Ravan approached the king-in-waiting, Kuber, and whispered in his ears, "It is time to establish a centralised power in Lanka. It is time to become Lankesh."

SAMVAD

"What is my vice?" Ram looked towards his master.

"You know it already," said Shiva, "One understands his weakness better than anyone else."

Ram pondered for a moment, "Anger."

Shiva smiled. He had just finished plugging the leakages in the cave. It had rained heavily the previous day. Arranging his straw mat on the floor, he was about to sleep. His muscles strained from the day's workout and he needed some rest. They had to be refreshed and ready for the next day's routine.

"Must have inherited it from my father," said Ram thoughtfully.

Shiva guffawed, "Even on his best days, Jamdagni's couldn't measure up to your temper."

"I need to conquer it then," said Ram in an enquiring tone.

Shiva nodded, "It is your greatest shortcoming, Ram. A man ruled by his vice falls the greatest depth."

Ram imagined himself enraged, and the picture which came to mind was not pleasant. Shiva looked towards his student. "Don't worry," he said, "It is because of your anger that I chose you."

Ram turned his attention to what his master had to say.

"A man's evil is a double-edged sword. It is his driving spirit. It makes him perform incredible feats. It keeps him adhered towards a purpose," said Shiva, the bluish tinge on his neck becoming darker, "Every human being is plagued with a certain degree of evil. There is no escaping it. In choosing my students, I look towards finding their driving force. The stronger it manifests, the better a student performs."

"Don't you think it harms me in some way?" Ram asked.

"Without the fire burning bright inside you, you wouldn't become the great warrior that I foresee. It is your anger towards any wrongdoing which keeps you on a righteous path. Embrace your evils. Don't fight it. Let it flow freely through your veins. But don't let it consume you. Let people remember Ram for more than just his temper. You need to master it, rather than letting it master you."

"What if it defeats me?" Ram asked.

Shiva took a deep sigh, "I have seen many succumbing to the evil which resides in their heart. Their greatest strength becomes the reason for their downfall. You need to redirect your evil rather than letting it **define** you. Don't let your reason surrender before it. The decision taken by a man intoxicated by his evil would be disastrous."

KUBER

"Is it any good?" Kuber asked as Vibhishan entered his room. The king was examining his crown. Since ascending the throne of Lanka, the crown had spent more time at the workshop than adorning the King's head. It started as a circlet of gold, with the teardrop shape of Lanka etched at its centre. Decked with multiple gemstones, a heavy golden dome to cover the head, thousands of diamonds studded across the tiny glistening expanse, multiple gold branches reaching outwards on the dome, symbolizing the various victories of the king, and rubies placed at its ends were some of the many modifications done to the crown.

"Isn't it too heavy for your head?" Vibhishan asked, holding the crown in his hands.

"Such is the weight of my responsibilities," Kuber said sarcastically with a deep sigh.

"Hope the King of Lanka is not drowned by his responsibilities." It was Ravan who entered the King's chambers. Looking at the crown, he said, "Honestly, I have never seen," his voice trailed off, "let alone imagined such a thing could exist."

"Want one for yourself?" Kuber asked Ravan.

"It suits you better," said Ravan before he hurried out, "I came here to check on you. We are getting late for the ceremony."

Vibhishan was still examining the helmet. Kuber wore his heavy bejewelled robes. He asked Vibhishan to help him with his crown.

Placing it on Kuber's forehead, Vibhishan asked, "Is this what we wanted from Lanka?"

"No," Kuber said, "More; much more."

The prosperity of the Lankan kingdom had increased by leaps and bounds under the leadership of Kuber. With trade monopolised across the whole route, the progress of Lothal and other such cities located along the western shores dimmed in comparison to Lanka.

"The ports are our cash cow. We should use them to improve the living standards of our citizens. I want every citizen to be provided with the basic requirements – health, food, education, shelter," Ravan, the newly anointed general of Lanka, declared from the podium. He was addressing a large assembly of Lankan subjects who had gathered to listen to the first family. The entirety of Lanka was celebrating the 'Freedom Day' – the day Ravan's army set foot in Lanka.

Vibhishan kept looking towards Kuber who was sitting next to him, as Ravan emphasised more on the state's duty towards its citizens.

"The treasury of Lanka belongs to its people and we will do whatever is in our capacity to ensure the well-being of our citizens," Ravan continued.

Kuber flinched when he noticed Vibhishan keenly observing him.

"I think they will have a good sleep this afternoon. Too many sweets for a day," he chuckled.

Ravan ended his speech to resounding huge applause. He returned to his seat alongside his brothers.

"Let the welfare of the citizens be taken care of by other people. You should not forget your primary duty, chief of the Lankan army. Build the strongest defence the world had ever seen," Kuber whispered in Ravan's ears when the minister of social welfare was announced as the next speaker.

***

With full control of Lanka in their hands, Kuber and his ministers put all their efforts into building and maintaining ports. But the overflowing treasury of Lanka attracted too much attention from other rulers. Lankan spies on the mainland had brought news in the past about conspiracies being hatched by ambitious kings to wrestle control from the hands of Kuber. In view of this, it was critical that the Lankan fort is guarded against any impending threat.

As per his brother's whims, Ravan busied himself in fortifying Lanka, but Kuber's disinterest towards the welfare of his subjects pricked at his conscience. Vibhishan and the other ministers kept bringing him worrisome accounts from the hinterland. While the rulers of Lanka lolled comfortably in their golden palaces, the masses lived in abject poverty. The tribes of Lanka considered the sea as their preserver which provided them fish; their staple food. None of the meals in a day were complete without its generous helping. But the advent of Kuber forced them to relinquish control over the seas. The waters, where fish were available in abundance and waited to be caught, were monopolised by the government. Now, the poor tribesmen had to buy them in limited supplies from the market. The government and its corrupt agents controlled the trade of almost all other commodities. The autonomous tribes of the past had no choice but to depend on the state for their survival.

Ravan, along with his fellow generals, was tasked with ensuring Lanka became impenetrable. He carefully studied its topography and tried to identify areas along the shores which were well-suited for the enemy to enter. The calm, sandy beaches caressed by the weak sea waves provided adequate sites for enemy ships to land. They were identified and guarded closely. Ravan identified the vantage points across the shores where he could line his archers. The rocky hills at a few places became observation points to view and identify any in-coming enemy activity, and alert the king. Walls and bunkers were built at various places to surprise the enemy with counterattacks. Ravan tried to utilize as much of the natural topography as he could for defence. He designed a military strategy manual that was distrib-uted among his generals. It divided the Lankan shores into different zones, and outlined the strategy for its defence.

But the people who were being protected by Ravan were still in jeopardy. Kuber's stinginess and insolence were despicable. It seemed his sole ambition in life was to amass as much wealth as he could, at the expense of others, without parting with any of it.

"We have so much money that every citizen can afford to eat and drink in gold vessels," the treasurer used to convey to Ravan.

Lanka and its wealth seemed to be a mere chimera. When Ravan looked around, he could see how impoverished the citizens of his kingdom were. He got news from certain quarters that people were dying of starvation and diseases, but the golden throne of Lanka was not the least bit shaken from its ground.

"It seems we haven't yet assumed the kingship of Lanka. We are mere merchants trading off the life sap of a foreign land," Vibhishan said to Ravan one day.

Ravan was getting frustrated by the impotency depicted by the Lankan throne. He had multiple discussions on this issue with Kuber, but to no avail. His elder brother always deflected the topic, telling him to concentrate on the duties prescribed by his designation.

"Is it because we are *Rakshashas*?" Ravan voiced his fears one day. It was a difficult statement to digest. Kuber had spent all his life with the *Rakshashas*.

"The king doesn't treat his people as his subjects; rather his slaves." Vibhishan too didn't seem sure.

***

A few workers at a port had been killed while trying to anchor a larger ship. Rather than paying a visit to the site to console the workers, Kuber sent soldiers to nearby villages to fetch able-bodied youths to replace the dead.

"We started this mission to become the mightiest rulers of *Bharatvarsh*, and not some filthy gold-digging merchants. History won't forgive us, Kuber," Ravan stormed into the king's chambers as soon as he heard about his order. His hands were tightly clamped on his sword.

"Money will buy you kingdoms, Ravan," Kuber said, removing the two gold coins he carried in his pocket. It was his lucky charm. He added with a smile, "and people too".

"You are a king now. You are one of the greatest explorers the world has ever seen. You changed your destiny through sheer grit," Ravan felt the sense of shame rising in his gut, "Don't let the greed swallow you."

Kuber looked at Ravan for a while. He could see his half-brother was genuinely concerned. He said thoughtfully, "Greed overtook me a long time ago, Ravan. It consumed me the day a young boy left Daman's farm teary-eyed. It was my greed that pushed me towards Lanka, and to explore the kingdoms further south. It is my life-force. It gives wings to my ambitions. Without it, we wouldn't have reached this far."

Ravan looked into his brother's eyes. He wanted to be sure his brother was speaking the truth. "The empire of Lanka is built on the shoulders of the locals. Don't betray their trust. Your 'life-force' is hurting their wellbeing."

Kuber chose to remain adamant, "I didn't create all this wealth, Ravan. It was already lying there for anyone's taking. I discovered it through my sheer ingenuity. These people you talk about, get scared so quickly on seeing a few soldiers with pointed maces. What do you expect from them? You want them to take advantage of my enter-prise? The same people who lacked the spine to do it themselves."

Ravan was startled to hear such words from his brother. Kuber continued, "I respect anyone who takes charge of his destiny and tries to change it. But what about these people? For centuries, they could not muster the courage to see what lay beyond the seas that surrounded them."

Ravan said calmly, "At least for the sake of humanity, let us not abandon them. We will educate them and maybe, one day, they might build up their courage like you."

Kuber laughed, "Humane towards these sub-humans? Don't you remember how we found these *Rakshasha* races living when we first came to this island? They are only fit to live in the jungles."

Ravan's hunch was right. Kuber's ignorance towards the well-being of his subjects ran much deeper. He stormed out of Kuber's room, hands still clenching the hilt of Chandrahaas.

After that incident, the warmth in Kuber and Ravan's relationship was extinguished like a candle's flame. Their paths crossed at the royal court, but Ravan found it difficult to exchange words with his older brother. Sub-humans, fit to live in jungles, lacking a spine – Kuber's insinuations were better left unheard.

"We have turned into tyrants against our *Rakshasha* brethren," he conveyed to Vibhishan one day. Ravan had just returned from visiting a cluster of villages located on the southern side of the island. He had gone there, accompanied by a few generals, to set up recruitment camps for the Lankan army. He had stayed away for a week, travelling to different villages, to inform the youth of the camps being set up. Most of the Lankan villages had been turned into a cesspool of poverty, disease, violence and degradation.

"We are failing our mother's words," said Ravan, "It is time to rise and present our worth."

Vibhishan was not surprised by Ravan's words. He was also aware of the living conditions of the Lankan subjects, but he was afraid to hear what Ravan might say next.

"Enough of the proud *Rakshashas* being ruled by a low-life *Yaksha*," said Ravan, his heart brimming with emotions.

Tears formed in Vibhishan's eyes. Time had been cruel to his family. The manifold dreams of his brothers had been achieved, but it had come at a great price. There was no looking back at that instant. "Do what you need to do, and I will always be with you," Vibhishan said hugging his brother tightly. He felt the warmth descending his neck. Ravan was crying softly.

***

A group of villagers had just finished a meeting with Ravan, and handed him a parchment. The infants and children were dying at a rapid rate; much higher than any kingdom Ravan had heard of.

'The future generation is responsible for carrying your name forward. It is the duty of any king to remain kindest to the generations to come,' his master's voice echoed in Ravan's ears.

"Help us, the blood of our blood," the oldest one in the group implored Ravan.

"We are not doing enough for our citizens, *Maharaj*," Ravan stormed into the *rangshala*, where Kuber was enjoying the performance of a group of singers visiting Lanka from Venad. Seeing Ravan seething with anger, Kuber dismissed the group.

"What brings you here, *Pradhan Senapati*?" Kuber asked, a languid smile playing on his face. They were used to addressing each other by their names.

Ravan handed him the parchment which contained the information brought forth to him. Kuber scanned it quickly before shifting his disinterested gaze towards Ravan.

"People are dying around us. What use is all this money we are making if we cannot take care of our people?" Ravan raged.

Kuber smiled, "It fills my coffers and merely eyeing it fills me with the greatest satisfaction. What will we achieve by saving them?"

Ravan stood astounded. If emperors of vast lands wore similar attitudes, the subjects would have no one, except God, to look to for help. A silent prayer escaped his lips directed towards his master.

"Once the children are old enough, they would work at our ports. Few would become servants at our palaces, while most of them would join our army. Our plan is to bring the mainland under our control. Don't forget that we have yet to initiate our campaign, which might live for years; if not decades. We need as many youths as possible to make our plan successful," Ravan tried to address the basest of Kuber's quality. He thought he could get Kuber to reluctantly loosen his purse strings if Ravan proved it might help him in hoarding more gold in the future.

"The *Rakshasha* women bear children like bitches in heat. I don't think we need to worry about that, Ravan. Even if a few die, there would be others ready to join our forces," Kuber said dismissively.

Ravan was taken aback. He hadn't expected such a venomous reply.

"Without proper health facilities, what would the parents do? Faced with a high mortality rate, they bear more children to increase their probability of survival," Ravan tried to drill some sense in Kuber. Clenching his teeth, he added, "You might have forgotten, but I am a *Rakshasha* too."

"Don't be so hard on yourself. You have the blood of a Brahmin flowing through your veins. It must have purified your ills by now," Kuber said in a sleepy voice.

Ravan felt a lump rising in his throat. The rancidity Kuber held for his race was too much to bear.

"You won the throne of Lanka through the efforts of the *Rakshashas*," said Ravan.

"I would have won it anyway. Don't forget it was my plan to conquer Lanka," said Kuber laughing loudly.

The time had come to choose between living in the shadow of his brother for his entire life, or take responsibility for the subjects of Lanka, Ravan thought. He understood his brother's attitude towards his subjects would be impossible to alter. 'After all, most of them were *Rakshashas*.'

***

Ravan went back to his room. Leaning against a wall was his sword, Chandrahaas.

"A perfect warrior is one whose weapon responds to an impulse, almost like it were a part of his own body. As years wean, imagining him without the weapon of his choice should become impossible. In people's minds, the weapon should become inseparable from his image," his master had said while handing him the Chandrahaas *Khadag*.

"This weapon will not only protect you against your enemies, but also guide you when the time comes," he had declared, as Ravan stood examining the sword.

"A time will come when you might be needed to restore the balance between good and evil. Evil needs to exist to make people realise the goodness within each other. But unless it is guarded, it can run havoc and ruin many lives. You, as my student, should help me guard it," said Shiva.

"And how do you know when you see evil?" Ravan asked.

Shiva smiled mysteriously, disarming any doubt that Ravan bore in his mind, "You will know."

He held his sword tight. 'Hope the hilt doesn't crack,' Ravan clenched his teeth in anger. Suddenly, something snapped beneath his fingers. 'I broke it,' he thought. Ravan murmured an apology to his master Shiva. Pressing the sword's hilt tightly had revealed an opening. Ravan looked through it and found a neatly folded parchment, smaller than the size of his thumb, placed inside.

He took it out. A single name was scrawled on it, 'Kuber'.

'Balance between good...,' his master's voice echoed in Ravan's mind. It was time for him to claim what was rightfully his. It was time for the rightful heir of Lanka's throne to assume his place. It was time for Ravan to stand and fight for the respect of the *Rakshashas*.

'The master holds all the strings,' he remembered how his father Vishrava used to refer to Shiva. Ravan ran his hands against the blade. It was no ordinary sword. The weapon grew on its owner. The hilt seemed to redesign itself, responding to the nook and crevices on Ravan's palm. It fitted him perfectly. Though the thickness of its blade revealed its weight, it had never really felt heavy to Ravan. But he had seen the difficulty faced by his brothers and fellow soldiers when they'd tried to lift it. The Chandrahaas somehow moulded with his body, and became one with him. Every time he wielded it, Ravan felt it was more like an extension of his arm.

The sword had protected him in many battles, but he sought its guidance at that moment. Lanka was his home and it was his duty to take care of its citizens. They belonged to the same race as him and by then, had fought alongside him in many battles. The overflowing treasury of Lanka shined a brilliant hue of yellow, far from the reach of its subjects who were bleeding red at multiple battlefronts.

JAMDAGNI

Jamdagni was breathing fire. He had suffered from periodic bouts of anger his entire life. The people around him were now used to his loud snorts, heavy breaths, and blood-red eyes; a phenomenon that occurred quite frequently with him. His wife, Renuka, was trying to calm him; as was her habit. She held his warm, sweaty hands with all the strength she could muster. At that moment, she had assumed it would be Jamdagni who would support her, but the seer was too angry to be of any use.

Renuka was writhing from labour pains and Jamdagni's mood was making it more difficult for her. It was their fifth child, and the cause of the most painful delivery. Seeing his wife under so much duress was making Jamdagni angry. His anger was directed towards the cause - the unborn child. With one hand on Renuka's bloated stomach, Jamdagni kept mumbling continuously; obscene words poured out in a constant rhythm. A silent prayer escaped Renuka's lips. She wearily hoped that the father would hold enough sense to not put a curse on his own child.

Jamdagni's *ashram* was on one of the lush green hills of Malana. Crossing the Gangotri, one of the most sacred places of the *Sanatanis,* and moving towards the north were the meandering desolate hills of Malana. The pilgrims had to combat freezing temperatures to visit Gangotri; the mouth of the mother Ganga – the river which bestowed vitality to the entire North. However, the enlightened ones and seekers of true knowledge, the *rishis,* moved further into the solitary expanse of the mountains; far from civilisation. The surrounding hills were dotted with multiple *ashrams* of renowned sages. It was only occasionally that a king or a *Kshatriya* chief would visit them - their wishes numerous and varied. While some childless couples came to wish for an offspring, others came to receive divine assistance against their enemies, while few others arrived with offerings, in return for the fulfilment of a wish from the past that had been granted. Malana was famous for the quality of its opium poppies. Many Shiva *bhaktas* like Jamdagni enjoyed a joint or two, whenever their strict schedule permitted them. Jamdagni took a personal interest in growing good quality opium poppies at his *ashram* - a hobby he had acquired from his master Shiva. He experimented with various methods of harvesting, and loved teaching his sons to take care of the plants.

"Collecting 'poppy tears' by scouring the ripening pods upwards involves patience, precision and concentration; the three qualities any seer or warrior needs to inculcate," the impatient Jamdagni would repeat to his sons. Like a doting father, he wanted them to become passionate about his hobby. He had filled a few parchments documenting the practice of growing and harvesting opium poppies, 'for the benefit of generations to come', as he would state.

In the last few hours, he had implored Renuka multiple times to take a few puffs from his *chillum*, but she had turned him down, frantically waving her hand. The surprise on Jamdagni's face at his wife's refusal was evident. The quick-fix solution was a cure for all ailments, as per Jamdagni. But his repeated suggestions fell flat before Renuka's wisdom. The child was on his way, and she needed all the strength she could muster to ensure safe delivery.

Soon, the nursemaids had Jamdagni leave the room. He waited outside, frantically pacing back and forth along the corridor, being consoled by his sons. Vasu, the eldest, knew his father well. He understood his whining wouldn't stop until their sibling was born. More than an hour had passed, and after a seemingly never-ending warp of time for Jamdagni, a maid came outside the room. She handed a small bundle wrapped in a white cloth to the father. It was a baby boy who was crying inconsolably.

"As if our father doesn't make enough noise in the house," Vasu said looking at his other siblings. Jamdagni kept staring at the child. He was trying to identify which features were similar to his.

"The frown," Vasu remarked. The child's forehead had deep markings, as if a permanent frown was embossed on him.

"Why were you so shifty throughout the procedure? See what you did to my child," Renuka teased Jamdagni as he walked inside, pointing towards the frown. He looked paler than she did.

"Have you thought of a name for him?" Jamdagni asked his family. They were amused, seeing how the hands of their father wouldn't stop trembling.

"Ram," they replied in unison. It was one of the popular names making the rounds those days.

"Rambhadra," Renuka said, as Jamdagni handed the baby back to her. The suffix she added meant 'gentle'. "It will help him maintain his composure," she said, unbeknownst of what the future held for her son.

***

Days turned into years, and the small patch on the hills of Malana, which had served as Jamdagni's abode, remained a joyous household. Being the youngest, Ram was pampered by his whole family. His four brothers - Vasu, Viswa, Brihudyanu, and Brutwakanwa were fiercely protective of him. Owing to his mother's love and affection, the youngest turned chubbier each day. The day's menu was decided based on his likings. The elder brothers had to be content with eating the food of his choice. But it was not an issue for the household.

Compared to Ram, the temperament of his brothers was quite gentle. Quick of temper, Ram got whatever he wanted easily. His favourite form of tantrum included him lying on the floor, while his face turned pink as he held his breath; something that came naturally to him. There was not a single toy that was denied to him by his parents, either voluntarily or forced by Ram's antics. His favourite ones were those designed in the likeness of popular warriors. Ram would be busy for hours, trying to make them fight each other. His brothers and father joined him whenever they found time. But that was the extent of his love for the weapons and battlefield.

While his four brothers dedicated themselves to learning weaponry from their father, Ram circled the *ashram* and watched them practice, holding one of his toys' strings in his hand. Whenever Jamdagni coaxed him to join the training with his brothers, a cloud of gloom descended on the child's face. It looked like someone was trying to steal his happiness. Rolling his fingers around the toy string, the boy kept shifting nervously on his feet while listening to the wise words of his father, a morose look residing on his face. Jamdagni would soon give up, unable to hold his rant for long in front of the shamefaced boy. Exhausted, he would return to train his other sons while Ram resumed his play.

"It is too easy for me," said the five-year-old Ram as his father approached him. Everyone was surprised to see him at the training ground, early one morning. It seemed the constant bickering with Jamdagni had finally paid off. They saw him trying to balance a large bow, which belonged to Vasu, on his shoulders.

"Aim for the target," Vasu said encouragingly, handing him a few arrows.

Ram tugged at the taut string with all his strength and shot at the target. The arrow landed midway after a short flight through the air. He looked around. Vasu and Jamdagni wore a satisfied look on their faces, while his other brothers were trying to suppress a smirk. Jamdagni placed another smaller bow in his hands and asked him to try again. Ram kept his body straight and pointed his bow a little upwards before shooting another arrow, which followed the same trajectory.

"Who tied Kamdhenu so close to the target? Thank God I noticed in time," Ram pointed towards the cowshed, which was at least fifty feet away from the scarecrow that was his target. Handing over his bow to Vasu, he ran towards the cowshed while his brothers laughed at his antics. A sigh of resignation escaped Jamdagni's lips. His hopes of training Rambhadra proved to be quite short-lived.

"At least one of your sons will do what a Brahmin ought to do. We will make him a *Chaturvedi*; one who is learned in all the four Vedas," Renuka said to her husband, looking at her youngest son fooling around. Her other sons were now busy training with heavy maces, smashing them against each other. The parents were content with the progress of their children. They knew they would be able to provide a happy household for their children.

***

Over the next few years, owing to the efforts of Renuka, and his own inclination, Ram developed an interest in Vedic scriptures and scientific texts. He discovered a ferocious appetite to devour the texts at a rapid pace. Stationing himself inside the house, he dedicated hours to reading the texts while his other brothers made it a point not to miss a single day of their training outdoors. Each one of Jamdagni's sons showed a hunger to excel at what they were doing. They learned and practiced for hours, training their body and mind. Though sometimes, seeing Ram poring over his books for hours on end, or watching Vasu practicing with his target late in the night, while covered in sweat, worried Renuka.

"We are not pushing our children to the limits, are we? I want them to lead a happy life," Renuka would say to Jamdagni.

Jamdagni looked towards Renuka's eyes, which were full of concern. He ran his hands through Ram's hair, who was busy solving a mathematics puzzle. "Living happily doesn't mean remaining stagnant. A man who always looks towards a higher purpose leads a fulfilling life. Remember Renu, our sons would face a lot of difficulties in their lives; for they are crafting the iron of their skills in the flames of time. They will emerge strong and resplendent and will be remembered for ages. But the fires of time are unforgiving. A man must sacrifice a lot before it yields anything. The best we can do, as parents, is to support them on their journey."

Soon, all the *shlokas* of the Vedas were at Ram's fingertips. During the nights, he held discussions with his parents on multiple interpretations of the verses from different scriptures. They were surprised to hear such opinionated questions being asked by a child. Even for Jamdagni and Renuka, Ram opened new vistas of enquiries. They didn't know that the Vedas could be understood from so many perspectives. Sometimes, they felt inadequate when answering his questions, but they encouraged Ram to continue to learn, observe, absorb and argue more.

Ram was progressing quite well in other subjects too. His skills in mathematics, geography, and history were simply unmatched, and far advanced when compared to the other children of his age. Even Vasu, who was many years older than him, consulted him when he needed his doubts cleared. He was even successful in creating his own puzzle book. Jamdagni and her other sons spent long hours splitting hairs over the book, but a lot of the puzzles remained unsolved. They consulted Ram multiple times for the solutions, but he remained tight-lipped about it. It was a small victory of his genius which he wanted to cherish.

***

That year, the winter arrived in full glory to Malana. The sun seldom visited the village, and the streets bore a deserted look, lying in wait for the summer when it would be filled with the milieu again. The village had been experiencing continuous snowfall for a few days. It had severely restricted the family's access to the outside world. But owing to their past experiences, they had prepared themselves to live comfortably throughout the season. Before the onslaught of the un-forgiving winter, Renuka had busied herself for a couple of months with stitching cotton blankets. Jamdagni had fixed the crevices in the house that could invite the cold wind in. The hearth in the cowshed was cleaned, and cows were tied next to it. The children collected as much dry wood as they could find; the most critical element to sur-viving the cold weather.

It was on one such wintery morning that there was a loud knock on the door. The family had not gotten any proper sleep the previous night due to the insistent mooing of Kamdhenu. She was tied with the other cows near the rudimentary hearth. That night, before going to bed, the parents had had a long discussion with Ram regarding the need for rituals to appease the Gods. They had not been expecting any visitor in the sub-zero temperatures so early in the morning. They had no neighbours for many miles around. Without any shelter, it was dif-ficult to survive even for a few hours outside.

After repeated nudging from Renuka, Jamdagni awoke with groggy eyes. Covering himself using a blanket, from head to toe, he went to the door and unbolted it. With a voice filled with gratitude, he called out to the visitor and prostrated himself before him. It was Shiva. The destroyer stood half-naked in his attire, the lionskin his only shield against the fierce winter, his trident firmly tied to his back. It seemed he had traversed a long distance to reach the *ashram*. His matted hair was covered in snow, and his neck had turned a pale shade of blue. He bent down to hold Jamdagni by his arms, before pulling him up and hugging him tightly. Though Jamdagni had taken care to cover himself, a cold shiver ran down his spine. The *adiyogi* felt too cold for comfort, but warm emotions flooded his heart as they stood reminiscing the past.

"Kailash has grown too cold this year," Shiva said, referring to his natural habitat, the Mount Kailash located north of Malana. For an ordinary human, it was impossible to survive even for an hour in the snow-clad mountains in such rough weather. Jamdagni knew few devotees who had desired to meet Shiva in person, and had lost their lives trying to conquer the difficult terrain of Kailash. A few times in the past, even Jamdagni had asked to accompany, much to Shiva's reluctance.

"You will find me whenever you need me. Besides, you have a family to take care of," he would say, refusing Jamdagni's imploring.

Shiva saw Jamdagni's children enjoying their cosy slumber. He closed the door behind him. The cold air outside had already disrupted the indoor warmth. Renuka too followed her husband's cue, and meekly moved to stand next to her husband to welcome Shiva.

"Very few people have the good fortune of meeting you in person. Our children haven't met you even once. Let me wake them up for you," she said, pointing towards an empty bed, "Please make yourself comfortable while I prepare some breakfast for you."

With a wave of his hand, Shiva dismissed Renuka's plea, "In its own time. There is no need to do any chores so early in the morning. I am guilty of disrupting yours and your children's sleep. I shall go check on the cattle. Jamdagni, meet me there when you are ready."

Jamdagni and Renuka knew Shiva always meant what he said. The *Bholenath* was not corrupted by human tendencies. There was no room for formalities in their conversations. They nodded in agreement, opening the door for Shiva.

"Will see you shortly there," said Jamdagni, before returning to his bed.

Jamdagni felt blessed for getting to know Shiva in his lifetime. Looking at him then, it seemed like he hadn't lost a year since they had last met. He and Renuka had been a recipient of his hospitality when they had decided to make Malana their home. It was one such winter when they had moved to this sleepy town. Not many people travelled that far up north, but Jamdagni, an ascetic, wanted to build his home as far from civilisation as possible. He had wanted to live a quiet and peaceful life, along with his wife. Renuka, though a princess by birth, had loved and respected her husband's idea, and accompanied him to the desolate, snow-covered lands.

Once they had reached Malana, they busied themselves with clearing the land to establish an *ashram*. The couple worked for days, from dawn till dusk, to build a warm cosy household. It was during that time that they met Shiva. They were surprised to see a reed-thin half-naked man roaming with abandon, in such harsh weather.

"You are new here?" he asked.

The couple nodded.

"A little help won't hurt," Shiva smiled.

Without any further enquiries, Shiva started levelling the land, which would serve as a cowshed in the future. For days, they continued working together. Shiva knew about a lot of things that came in handy during the rough weather. He made the couple's stay as comfortable as he could till their home was completed. At nights, he would light a small bonfire to help them sleep comfortably. During the day, he got them acclimated to the surroundings. He showed them places where they could farm for freshwater, wild fruits, shrubs, and vegetables. He helped Jamdagni plant a small vegetable garden in the *ashram*. He also taught them the best techniques to store grains for a long time without letting it rot.

Jamdagni developed an instant liking to him. Before moving to Malana, he had not given much thought to how difficult it might be to survive there. For the few days that they had stayed there without Shiva's assistance, Jamdagni doubted whether his whims had landed his wife in a soup. But after Shiva appeared, all his apprehensions melted, and he became confident that he would be able to take care of his family. Not only that, Shiva also helped the couple to cope with the utter gloom brought forth by such weather. Shiva had a congenial personality that easily rubbed off on others. His stories kept Renuka and Jamdagni engrossed for hours; details about ferocious demons, ravishing mermaids, gentle half-beasts were beyond their imagination. But there was something else that surprised them immensely. On the days that Shiva lived with them, they had never seen him cover himself up with anything, other than the old, shrivelled-up lion skin. He took to the cold weather as a fish takes to the water.

Once a functioning *ashram* was built, Shiva participated with Jamdagni in teaching a few of his students, who had travelled from far-off places. Jamdagni's reputation as a learned seer was well-established in *Bharatvarsh*, and the wards of rich Kshatriya chiefs and kings undertook the long arduous journey to reach his *ashram*. With Shiva by his side, teaching the students became an enlightening journey even for Jamdagni. His students received a lot more than what they had bargained for. Jamdagni found great pleasure in joining his students, and listening wide-eyed to Shiva's philosophical renderings. Even the Vedas seemed incomplete in their knowledge before Shiva.

"What is your caste?" Jamdagni asked Shiva once. Shiva laughed gently hearing his question.

"Like everyone, I have the qualities of all the four *varnas*," replied Shiva.

"I believe you to be a Brahmin. Looking at your knowledge, I assumed you were a son of an accomplished sage," Jamdagni ventured further.

Shiva guffawed, "Your birth doesn't guarantee anything. I know, therefore I am. The closer you are to the true knowledge, the better a Brahmin."

Jamdagni looked at him amused. He had been expecting such a reply from Shiva. Any human who held such great knowledge of the Vedas could be anything but entangled in the web of castes.

Within a few days, Jamdagni got to see another side to Shiva. A few of the tribes who had been living around Malana for centuries were known for their demonic tendencies. They would loot, maim or kill anyone who tried to lead a peaceful life in those hilly areas. Shiva was adept at wielding his trident and saved the family, not once, but quite a few times from the scourge of such tribes. He was an exceptional warrior; better than anyone Jamdagni had seen till date. His trident seemed to be a part of his body. Seeing him in action was like watching a mesmerising dance. The enemies who came in hordes against the supposedly helpless seer were slaughtered in a matter of seconds. While Jamdagni himself was proficient in handling weapons, he never had to raise them in the presence of Shiva. The decapitated bodies were stacked on top of the other around which Shiva's lithe form swayed like a trained acrobat. Untouched by his enemies, he made them pay for their sins.

"Now you know how good a Kshatriya I am," the *adiyogi* said in an emphatic tone. He had just fought off another swarm of menacing aggressors.

"I want to be at least half as good a Kshatriya as you," Jamdagni said laughing. It was on that day that he accepted Shiva as his master. Placing his palms on his feet, he asked Shiva to take him as his student. Shiva readily agreed.

For the next couple of years, Shiva remained in Jamdagni's *ashram*, and taught him the art of defending oneself with different weapons. Shiva's techniques were unique. Jamdagni enjoyed learning about them and their sessions together.

"Where did you learn all this?" Jamdagni asked, while Shiva taught him how to tackle a warrior equipped with a mace.

"There is no better teacher than solitude. Kailash taught me everything. Looking down from a mountain, everything we hold dear looks so small and fragile. Quite a few things become invisible to the eye. It makes you realise the inconsequence of human civilisation, and motivates you to set greater goals that set you apart. It is only through isolating yourself from others, that you realise your true potential," said Shiva.

Within a year, Shiva made Jamdagni an expert at swordplay. The Kshatriya kings who came to seek his blessings were impressed by his prowess. Many offered him the role of a head priest in their court, and a mentor to their princes, but Jamdagni declined. He was in no mood to leave Malana and return to the plains.

"I have found Shiva," he would say, "and no one would leave him once they have found him."

Earlier, Jamdagni had been worried about the safety of his family, but a few years under Shiva's tutelage had freed him from any such stress. Not just his family, Shiva's training had ensured Jamdagni's capabilities were more than adequate to also protect others who inhabited Malana. The evil which surrounded Malana had begun to dread his name.

***

After completing his ablutions, Jamdagni went to the cowshed with Ram tagging along. Shiva was busy putting dry wood into the cold hearth. The cows had left their usual places to cope with the freezing weather. They were huddled together in a corner; the little ones lodged in the middle, sheltered by the pack. Jamdagni helped Shiva to relight the fire. Shiva looked at the fat child accompanying his father, who stood waiting for instructions. With age, Ram had grown solemn and more composed; at present, his childhood frown appeared to portray a serious intent towards finishing the job at hand. Shiva observed his forehead for a bit.

"He too seems to have the third eye," he said smiling. Shiva's own metaphorical third eye was famous among the masses. The harbinger of destruction, Shiva had a distinct frown adorning his forehead. A slight twist and the person facing him knew that he had invited a burning fury upon himself.

"I assume you are the tutor for your sons?" Shiva enquired.

"They are quite talented," Jamdagni said referring to his children, "Adaptive to the circumstances, they learn things quickly. But I'm quite sure none of them would turn out to be better than me."

"Why is that?" Shiva asked.

"Because I had a better teacher," said Jamdagni. The fire was burning bright. Jamdagni directed Ram to bring the cows back to their designated places.

"So, what have you learned from your father?" Shiva asked as Ram tied the cows back to their places. Ram stood in silence, looking at Shiva nonplussed.

"If only," Jamdagni laughed, "the pen was his sword."

Shiva looked intently at the boy waiting for his reply, but he didn't receive any. He asked again, "What are all that you have read, son?"

"Vedas, Upanishads, Aranyakas, all the Smritis, you name it. I think he has completed the volumes on *bhugol, itihaas* and *ankganit*; the ones which you had given me. He hasn't left any subject untouched. Now, he has started writing his own books," Jamdagni said, referring to the puzzle book Ram was quite proud of. Unable to hide the tinge of pride in his voice, he said, "It is only my limited collection of texts that is proving to be a hindrance."

"I think the child can speak for himself," Shiva looked sharply at him. Jamdagni had not been expecting such a response. He shifted back nervously, bringing Ram to the forefront.

"How should one lead his life?" Shiva asked.

Ram pointed at the hearth, "Comfortably in a warm house, with equally warm relations. Around nature, in harmony with others. With a clean heart bereft of blemishes, a clear mind, and soul. Anything that seeks to destroy this well-balanced tranquillity should be challenged."

"What books have you read to date?" Shiva repeated his earlier question.

"Not too many. I have just started," Ram was wiser than Shiva had thought.

"Are you keen to learn about warfare?" Shiva asked.

The question seemed unrelated. Jamdagni looked at Shiva perplexed. Ram had never shown any interest in learning to handle weapons since his childhood.

"Yes, I think I am ready now," Ram answered with conviction, to his father's surprise. That particular morning was full of surprises for Jamdagni. His master had visited him after so many years, in this frigid weather, and now, his son who had spent a few years teaching himself from books, had expressed his interest in learning weapons.

Never had he thought that his love for the scriptures would somehow lead him to this path.

While going through the texts, Ram had held several discussions with Jamdagni, and quite a few times, Shiva's name had cropped up.

"Who is Shiva?" Ram had once asked Jamdagni.

"Shiva knows everything. He controls everything. He is the most knowledgeable amongst us all, more than anyone who will reside on this earth in the future. It's his knowledge that makes him all-powerful," Jamdagni said reverentially.

"Can he see the future as well?" Ram knew of many sages who claimed as such.

"Shiva works in mysterious ways. From what I know, he can predict the course of the future," said Jamdagni.

"Is there no free will if Shiva controls everything?" asked Ram.

"It is we who must decide what to choose. But Shiva seems to understand our psyche well," said Jamdagni.

From that day, Ram had been drawn to such an intriguing personality. Now, standing before him was the master himself; his father's teacher. Shiva knew all the right questions. 'There are so many things I can discuss with him,' felt Ram.

Shiva looked at his former student. "With your permission, I would like for Ram to accompany me to Kailash."

Shiva's request took Jamdagni by surprise. Though Shiva was the best teacher anyone could get during his formative years, he was not too sure about his choice of the student.

"My other sons are far more skilled than Ram in using weapons. I have trained them myself. Ram is the youngest and has never been too keen on joining them during their training. You can take any one of them with you," he said.

"An archer skilled in shooting targets is not enough. Your actions should be directed towards a sense of purpose. Even at such a young age, I believe Ram knows what he stands for, and what he wishes to fight for. He understands the difference between good and evil. The glory he will bring to your family will surpass what could you have ever imagined, Jamdagni," Shiva seemed to be quite impressed by his newfound student.

Jamdagni knew Shiva never spoke things lightly. His thoughts have always been a mystery to him. Only Shiva knew how he had deciphered so much about Ram, in such a short time. The trio talked for a while before they went back inside the house. Renuka had been waiting for them as breakfast was ready. Jamdagni's family sat with Shiva to enjoy the warm meal. It was then that Jamdagni informed Renuka about Shiva's request. The smile on her face dropped as soon as she heard it.

"Ram wouldn't survive a day at Kailash," she looked teary-eyed towards Shiva.

"Mother, I will be back sooner than you think," Ram tried to console her.

"You are just a child. Leave your important decisions to us," she snapped. Jamdagni came forward to hug her.

"Don't you see he hasn't ever stepped outside this house, let alone go to Kailash?" she said to her husband.

The argument between husband and wife continued for an hour, during which time, Shiva chose to remain silent. It was a private matter, and besides, the meal before him was quite delicious. He decided to focus on the food for a while. Coaxed and prodded by her husband and sons, Renuka remained adamant about not allowing Ram to leave, but the group didn't give up on trying to convince their mother.

"How many disciples of Shiva do you know? There are only a few who have been blessed to witness him at such close quarters. We can't let go of the opportunity being offered to our child. As parents, we should think about what is best for our child's future," Jamdagni tried to reason with his wife.

"What will he get out of it? You know he is no good at using weapons," a teardrop escaped Renuka's eyes.

"I will make him the best warrior the world has ever seen," Shiva said. He was the last one to leave the breakfast table. Washing his hands, he added in jest, "Though, I must add, I am not sure whether it is my realism that is trying to answer your doubts or the optimism this sumptuous meal has induced in me. While I ask for your son to accompany me as my student, I feel like I should become yours in return. There is a lot, in terms of culinary skills, to learn from you."

Renuka was immensely devoted to Shiva. She looked into his sincere eyes and knew he meant what he said. It was Ram's good fortune that Shiva had shown faith in his talent. With sorrowful eyes, she asked for a day while the family bid farewell to their youngest son.

"Take as many days as you want," said Shiva, "I understand how difficult it can be for a mother. However, I would like to make a small request. I hope you'll allow me to sleep in the cowshed during this time. I don't want to trespass on your family's privacy."

There was no point arguing with Shiva. He could not be coaxed into changing his decision. Renuka nodded in affirmation and went outside to feed the cows. She needed some time alone to prepare herself to part with her youngest son.

The next day was spent packing Ram's luggage. Renuka didn't want Shiva to spend many nights in the cowshed in such weather. She took great pains to ensure Ram had everything he might need. With no desire to trouble the hearts of her loved ones, she slipped into the kitchen whenever she felt like crying. She had understood her sons had every right to choose what was best for them, and her emotions would not become a hindrance in achieving it. Shiva spent his day at the training ground with the other children, teaching them a few tricks about weapon handling.

Early the next morning, he readied himself for the travel, which would last for a few days. Giving a warm hug to Jamdagni and bidding farewell to his family, he started towards Kailash on foot with Ram.

"You came here just for this purpose?" Jamdagni asked Shiva, tightly embracing Ram one last time. The question had troubled him the night before.

Shiva turned and smiled, "No, Kailash had turned quite cold this winter."

After a flurry of hugs and goodbyes with the members of the family, Shiva started prodding through the seemingly never-ending thick layer of snow, carrying the unusually heavy backpack of Ram. He looked at Ram and forgot about the weight of the luggage he was carrying. Ram seemed to be carrying a heart heavier than the backpack. The sorrowful eyes of Ram and his parents reminded Shiva to fulfil his promise to Renuka; to make Ram the greatest warrior the world had ever seen.

SAMVAD

"Shiva is not so easy to please. The task you are undertaking is equivalent to moving Mount Kailash itself," Ravan tried to mime the voice of an old sage who had tried to advise him.

"And you did move it." It was Nandi, a close associate of Shiva, "Living next to Kailash for years is not an easy task. Facing the harsh weather and knowing that the master is still not impressed by your antics can be quite discouraging. But you persisted. You kept pursuing Shiva to make him your teacher, and it ended well for the both of you after all."

Shiva was listening to the discussion. He had been worried about a few qualities of his new student. He had won over Shiva through his perseverance. While he was a quick learner and performed splendidly at any task, his heart didn't seem to be still.

"It seems you want to impress the world with your prowess," Shiva said worryingly.

"Is being ambitious a flaw?" Ravan asked.

"All your actions and energies should be guided towards making this world a safe place where everyone can grow and live to their fullest potential without fear. Ambition is good till the time it is directed towards this goal. The lives of others should not be trampled upon by one's ambition. Unbridled ambition does more harm than good," Shiva said.

Ravan was not convinced, "It was only my ambition that had kept me glued to this path for so long. Let me know if you can find someone who has shown greater devotion and is more worthy of becoming your student. I will try to surpass him too. There is no greater glory one can attain in his life than being taught by Shiva himself."

It was true that it was difficult to find someone as dedicated as Ravan. He had given up on worldly pleasures, and like his master, had made Mount Kailash his abode. Very few were able to reach that place, let alone survive.

"What brought you here?" asked Shiva.

"I wanted to prove that a *Rakshasha* can do it; that he can be better than the most learned Brahmin and the most powerful Kshatriya," he said.

"And when would it end?" Shiva asked worriedly.

"Till *Aryavarta* treats us as equals," Ravan said in a determined voice.

It would be a difficult task, from what Shiva knew. This student of his was already ready to turn the world upside down.

"A bit of churning is always good for the world," Nandi remarked laughingly.

RAVAN

Lanka, a small decrypt island, lying towards one end of the main-land, had been transformed into the cynosure for all eyes since the advent of Ravan. The *Rakshasha* tribes, who had been disparate and fought amongst themselves, now took pride in being a citizen of one of the richest kingdoms in the world.

"A state is built upon its people and it is for the people that we need to prosper," declared Vibhishan, the general of the Lanka army, from the parapet of the palace of Lanka. Standing next to him was the new king of Lanka, Ravan, who looked benignly over the expanse of his kingdom. Forcing Kuber out of his throne had not been that difficult. The army comprised mainly of *Rakshashas* who held their commander in great esteem. The locals who formed the majority were already dis-traught over Kuber's ways. Having fought many battles alongside their brave general, they were quite loyal to his commands.

"I don't want to cause any scene," Ravan remembered telling Kuber, the Chandrahaas in his hand shining brilliantly, "The throne of Lanka belongs to its people, but your control over it is inhibiting their growth. It would be better if we settle this matter amicably. You are my brother and I will make sure you live comfortably for the rest of your life."

Kuber stood shamefaced, surrounded by the soldiers who, a few hours before, were answering to his commands. Never had he imag-ined that these puny *Rakshashas* would one day grow enough courage to revolt against him. But he was about to be dragged away from his throne like an ordinary prisoner.

"As a king, tell me Ravan, did I betray you or your brothers in any way?" asked Kuber.

Ravan looked icily into the eyes of his king, "No, but you betrayed the trust of the *Rakshashas.* You hurt their pride."

"Their pride or yours?" Kuber laughed.

Ravan ignored his insinuations. "We stood strong against all your adversaries, obeyed your commands to the dot, and what did we get for our efforts? The person entrusted with the fruits of our labours never bothered to leave his ivory tower to take care of our families and our miseries."

A mocking smile played on Kuber's face, "Why do I have a feeling that you are not addressing me, but rather this motley group of yours? You have turned preachy, Ravan."

"Tell me, Kuber, what plans did you have for the treasury of Lanka, envied by even the largest kingdoms of the world?" Ravan asked.

"I think we discussed that many a time. I wanted it to be utilised to fortify Lanka. This is one of the simplest rules of kingship, Ravan, a department in which you have limited experience," Kuber said snidely. "Don't you see how people travelling from far-off lands on their large ships are awestruck by the beauty of our palace? Don't you see their eyes darting back and forth, their minds making quick calculations as ships keep turning up to our ports while paying a hefty fee? What stories do you think they carry back to their homelands? They talk about the quick strides Lanka is making towards wealth. The palace of Lanka is envied by all; a structure worthy of the Gods. We need to provide iron-clad security for this small island of ours. We need to fortify it and that costs quite a lot of money."

"Fortified for whom? For the hungry souls who look towards the sky to satisfy their parched throats?" roared Ravan, "From today, the treasury of Lanka will be open to its people. We will invest in our citizens' future. The empire of Lanka had dithered from its objective, but now, it is our duty to bring it back on its righteous path."

Kuber removed his crown and handed it to Ravan. He knew he won't be able to find support for his cause once Ravan had turned against him. Tears formed at the corners of his eyes. He turned to view the throne of Lanka one last time. The heavily studded golden seat awaited its next ruler. Pointing towards it, he whispered in his brother's ears, "Power corrupts all, Ravan. Wait for it to happen. Let us see what it brings forth in you. For now, you might be moved by the welfare of the people. Wear this helmet for long and it will start guiding your vision. You will be wearing the curse of the gold."

***

A conglomerate of small islands had been worrying Ravan for months now. It stood towards the west of Lanka and had refused to surrender despite several skirmishes.

"I hereby commit my whole life for the pride of the *Rakshashas*. Let the golden age of Lanka begin," Ravan had announced, before launching attacks at multiple fronts soon after he had assumed the throne of Lanka. He anointed Vibhishan as commander-in-chief of the Lankan army.

With a new king on the throne, Lanka relentlessly pushed his objective to extend its influence. Many kingdoms were brought to their knees by his *Rakshasha* kin. Dandaka *van* was by far the largest. A dense jungle, Dandaka was ruled by Khara, a cousin of Ravan who had to defeat many mighty kings in the south to establish his influence.

"For centuries, *Rakshashas* have been far removed from the mainstream. We have tried to learn and emulate the ways of others. Many among us have proven themselves to be more courageous and skilled than the brave Kshatriyas. There are also those who are more learned than the wise Brahmins. I, Ravan, born to a Brahmin father, was never considered one. Even in this patriarchal society where your father's name takes precedence, I am only known by the *Rakshasha* identity of my mother. Since it is difficult to erase our identities as *Rakshasha*, let us embrace it. Let us dedicate our lives to the glory of our clan. By wresting power from others, we will establish the hegemony of the *Rakshashas*." Ravan had established his ideals as wanting to become the most powerful ruler in the history of the *Rakshashas*.

"It is the lack of iron that is making our citizens sick," Ravan's chain of thoughts was broken by the voice of his brother, Vibhishan.

Ravan saw the *raj vaidya* accompanying Vibhishan. Extending one's influence on new territories brings new people, along with their problems. A few of the forest-dwelling non- *Rakshashas* tribes in Dandaka *van* had suffered from a mysterious disease for generations. It made their hands and feet swell, causing joint pains, and lowered their life expectancy.

"They are a blot on our empire. Such weaklings!" Ravan exasperated.

Vibhishan smiled wryly. He was not sure how to answer his king.

"We would need more funds for our research, *Rajan*," the *raj vaidya* said, "it is due to some impurities in their blood. The patient's body lacks sufficient energy to perform vital functions."

"We have already invested so much in this research, *Maharishi*," Ravan looked worried, "and with no progress to show."

"No progress," the *raj vaidya* exclaimed, "are you unable to see the efforts of my team? We have been dedicatedly studying this disease for the last two years."

"But what did you achieve in these two years, sage?" said Ravan, "I funded it as my initiative, recruited the best health officials, sent explorations to far-off lands to bring medicinal herbs and provided you with the best equipment. Do you know how much it costed our treasury?"

"What is more valuable than the lives of the citizens of Lanka?" the *raj vaidya* asked, "All the health officials you hired have put their minds and hearts into searching for the solution to this disease. All the medicinal herbs are being experimented on, to provide the best concoction. All the equipment is being utilized."

"I am tired of your lamentations," Ravan boomed. The old frail fellow paled on witnessing his king. He had recently turned ninety and was the oldest member of the Lankan court. No one, not even the erstwhile King Kuber, had ever been rude to him. Ravan felt embarrassed for losing his temper. Deflecting the topic, he turned towards Vibhishan, "What is the news from the war front?"

"The Lakkadives," Vibhishan said, referring to the island cluster towards the west, "are still refusing to accept our dominance."

"Then is the general of Lanka sitting idle? Are you so disempowered that a small group of villages will stand against us now?" said Ravan.

"We need more weapons," said Vibhishan, "much better weapons."

"What are you waiting for?" Ravan said excitedly, "the *Rakshashas* have entrusted their faith in you, my brother. And you tell me you are struggling to buy weapons? The whole Lankan treasury is at your feet. Send your best soldiers, but bring Lakkadives under our control."

Vibhishan kept looking towards the *vaidya* as Ravan spoke. Since becoming king, Ravan's sole purpose had been to bring more territories under his control. The *Rakshashas* had been engaged in numerous battles.

"You can continue with your research, *vaidya*," Ravan turned towards the court doctor, "but consider that the palace of Lanka had already helped you enough. I don't see any money left to spare for the research."

The end of the court funding would mean two years of hard work going down the drain. It would be quite difficult to keep the team of researchers together at that point. They would need to start looking for better avenues.

"Healthy subjects make better warriors," the *vaidya* said trying his luck.

"We have quite a few healthy *Rakshashas* in our army," Ravan said dismissing the doctor.

The *raj vaidya* nodded and left the court. 'Time acts in strange ways,' the vaidya thought, 'Lanka still awaits a ruler who doesn't lose his mind after wearing the crown.'

***

"We have been facing a lot of resistance from a few kingdoms," said Vibhishan.

"And our brave general continuously fails to overcome them," Ravan said snidely.

"They are being assisted by a mighty empire," said Vibhishan.

"Mightier than Lanka?" Ravan felt his anger rising.

The other courtiers watched the conversation with terrified expressions. Such scenes in the court had become a regular occurrence by then. War was the only constant people witnessed since Ravan's ascension. Most of the government welfare projects had been halted by that point. There was not enough money in the treasury to be diverted towards them. The local administration too showed disinterest towards such initiatives. Their work didn't have much visibility in the eyes of the royal court.

Guided by his internal affairs minister Kumbhkarn, the king had undertaken quite a few initiatives early in his reign. Education was made compulsory for everyone, with public *gurukulas* opened in every village. Health clinics were revamped and provided with free drugs. Wells and canals were dug across the island to help in agriculture. But slowly, wars started eating into the state's budget. Armies were now the biggest source of employment for the Lankan citizenry. Recruitment camps dotted the entire map of the country, always hungry for fresh recruits.

"I think I have become busier than you had been when our brother assumed the throne," Vibhishan quipped looking at Kumbhkarn. The internal affairs minister was resting in his chambers; an activity that took most of his time during the day.

"I'm not sure about others, but it seems 'the golden age' has arrived for me," Kumbhkarn was still full of mirth.

"So, what are you currently focusing on?" Vibhishan asked.

"The young ones are being cared for by you, which leaves me with the wrinklies and cripples," he said laughingly.

A few months ago, the *raj vaidya* had been executed in public view on charges of corruption. He was accused of nepotism and running a shady non-profitable project which siphoned money. The *gurukulas* around the country had sent many petitions to the palace complaining about the dearth of staff. Quite a few of them had to close their operations due to lack of it. The monsoons had been quite cruel over the last few years and many areas were still flooded. People thronged the local state offices, but the officials were not able to provide any satisfactory answers; their salaries too were delayed for months.

They met success at various fronts under the leadership of Vibhishan but the Lakkadives remained belligerent. Ravan called the entire royal court to a meeting to strategize his upcoming battle plan. Vibhishan, weariness etched on his face, entered the court. The commander of the Lankan army was weighed down by his duties. 'Sometimes, while I stand on the battleground, I wonder what my primary goal should be; to kill more enemies or save my own soldiers,' Kumbhkarn remembered him reflecting. Lanka was continuously adding names to its list of enemies.

"King Kartavirya Arjun of Mahismati has formed alliances with many southern states. The sovereignty of Lakkadives is supported by him," Vibhishan opinionated on reasons for the delay in capturing the island state.

"It will take days for Mahismati to react. Last time I heard, the army of Lanka was adept at surprising its enemies," Ravan said sharply.

"That is why we won when we started the campaign. Now, the whole *Bharatvarsh* is aware of our ambitions," Vibhishan kept his tone soft, wondering how far removed the king was from reality.

"So, should we give up on Lakkadives?" roared Ravan.

"We are doing our best, King Ravan. But I am afraid forcing these kingdoms into submission might lead to a full-blown war against Mahismati," said Vibhishan.

"I am not afraid of it. Put as many people on the front as possible. Equip them with the most devastating weapons. It seems you lack conviction regarding the strength of your army. I pity the soldiers who fight under such leaders," scoffed Ravan.

The chief of the Lankan army was not ready to be rebuked publicly.

"Kartavirya Arjun is a brave warrior. He leads his army in every battlefield," Vibhishan retorted in front of the other courtiers who were too fearful to intervene.

Since assuming the throne, Ravan hadn't led a single war himself. He looked sharply at Vibhishan. He hadn't been expecting such a reply. His brother had turned quite sombre since assuming the leadership of Lankan defences. The furrows on his forehead had grown deeper. He held no doubts about Vibhishan's loyalty. It was the first time Vibhishan had lost his cool.

"Is the general of Lanka good at anything apart from pointing fingers?" Ravan asked in a dispassionate voice, "Let Mahismati declare war against Lanka. This time, I will commandeer the soldiers with you."

He didn't have to wait long. Arjun seemed to be harbouring similar ambitions. The lust for power glowed brightly in both their minds. Mahismati and Lanka were about to get involved in the most epic battle of all times.

Vibhishan gave a quick glance to Kumbhkarn, who sat lazily on his seat, indifferent to the court proceedings. Bowing before the king, he withdrew himself respectfully from the court. The general returned to the tired army of Lanka to ask them to prepare for another war.

<u>ARJUN</u>

Dawn was yet to break when Kartavirya Arjun left his bed; a bit darker than when he usually woke up. He looked out the window in a corner of his room. The sky was clear, and all was silent; except for an owl squeaking in a distance. The torches still burned at the parapet and he saw a few guards sleeping at their post. The temple marked by the line of morning visitors waiting for the gates to be opened was still enveloped by darkness.

He closed his eyes and let the cold wind caress his cheeks. The sound of the water sloshing against the banks felt like music to his ears. The cool, damp air filled his nostrils and refreshed his senses. He looked at the view of the waters of the Narmada, flowing past the deep rocky channel. The mother of the Haiyaya kingdom, Narmada provided everything its subjects needed. Every morning, their king prayed in silence for her continued benevolence. Since childhood, Arjun had heard thousands of odes dedicated to the glory of the river Narmada. Several peans of romance had been written on its banks which became popular in the kingdom of Mahismati. The gurgling sounds of the river soothed his nerves and transported him to his youth. Not long ago, a small thatched hut at the banks of the mother Narmada served as his home. He had spent many youthful years near its crystal-clear waters, learning from a few of the greatest teachers of *Bharatvarsh*.

A small smile curled his lips as he remembered his journey. He had always envied the ascetics. To seek knowledge, they renounced everything in search of it. Everything held dear by people turned into dust in their journey towards greatness.

"You know the scriptures better than anyone in our kingdom," the

head priest used to tell him. But it had not always been the same.
King Kartavirya sat on the throne of Mahismati when his court was
visited by an adolescent. Arjun, a few years younger to him, was sitting beside his father. As was his habit, Kartavirya bought his son to
watch the court proceedings every day; a much-needed respite for his
mother.

Arjun saw his father - his head bowed, and palms joined in a reverential *namaskar* - finding his way through the throng of courtiers greeting the juvenile. He sat, watching the crowd; their devoted eyes and
cheery faces conveyed the respect they held towards the sage in saffron robes.

Arjun saw his father washing the sage's feet. The perfumed water was
poured into a golden bowl after use and placed on the king's throne
as a mark of respect. Kartavirya whispered into the ears of a few of
his attendants, who scampered away, only to return with plates full
of valuables. The sage dismissed it with a wave of his hand. Few of
the ministers consulted the sage regarding the auspicious dates to
launch a few of the state programs. For the next couple of hours, the
court of Kartavirya remained busy in attending to the sage.

"Who was he?" asked Arjun after the sage left, and his father had returned to his seat.

"One who knows all," said Kartavirya, his eyes still reflecting his dedication towards the sage.

"Why didn't he take any jewels or valuables which were offered?"
Arjun said, visibly confused. It took an hour for several attendants to
dress the prince of Mahismati every morning. Different combinations
of rings, armlets, diadems, necklaces and brooches were tried and
spurned. Arjun's tantrums reached its peak as the attendants tried to
appease him with their selection of jewellery. He was quite particular
about what he wore. But none of it held any value in the eyes of the

sage.

"He would have refused even if the king offered him his kingdom," the priest of Mahismati who was sitting next to the king's dais, echoed Kartavirya's thought.

"Why?" asked the child. His left cheek had started twitching.

Kartavirya laughed, "You are too young for all these big talks. It is quite late already. Let me finish attending to the court. Your mother must be waiting. She will give me dreadful warnings if I turn up late. We need to take you to the local market today. A few cloth merchants from other kingdoms are exhibiting their wares. You need some new clothes."

'But the sage was almost my age and he would never have wanted such a thing,' Arjun thought, as his father got busy with the court proceedings. The twitch had turned into a visible trembling. He looked at the large ruby he was wearing on his finger. The shine seemed to have dimmed a bit since that morning. A tinge of jealousy rose in his gut. He wanted to command the same respect he saw in the eyes of the other courtiers and his father for the sage.

***

Arjun was one of the mightiest kings of his age. 'Destroyer with a thousand arms', Sahasrabahu Arjun, was the dreaded name his enemies, who had been reduced to a smaller number on account of being killed or befriended, had given him. The relentless campaigns of the Mahismati army had struck fear in the opposition's heart. It was the largest army the country had ever seen. The king was also a ferocious warrior on the battlefield. His chariot, considered divine by many, was a work of art. Built of pure gold and driven by ten horses, it was large enough to accommodate half a dozen people. Its wheels, fitted with thick, long, strongly welded spears, caused havoc in the enemy camps whenever Arjun rolled by in his chariot.

Ever since he assumed the reigns of Mahismati, Arjun's kingdom had spent much of its time waging wars against other empires. Even though he was discouraged many times by his generals, Arjun would put his life at risk during the wars. Impatient for a finish, he would ask his charioteer to follow his lead while unbolting a horse. Slashing his sword or wielding his specially designed mace, the king would breeze through the enemy ranks on his horse. Sometimes, it became quite difficult to gauge who was raining greater damage - the king or his chariot.

The king was also a collector. Arjun's penchant for gold was not hidden from anyone. Since childhood, he had seen kings and princes of large empires coming to Mahismati at his father's invitation. Decked in gold from head to toe, these kings could turn anyone green with envy on seeing their wealth. Arjun, sitting next to his father, would stare for hours, wide-eyed at the rich attire they wore.

"A king's strength is measured by the amount of gold residing in his treasury," his father Kartavirya would often say.

His sword bore the royal insignia of the Haiyaya, the clan of his ancestors, which had been passed down through the generations. It was modified to have an intricately designed, golden hilt studded with gemstones. The insignia too was made bigger using the shiny metal. In the battlefield, his gold-plated armour shone brilliantly under the sun. The enemy knew from a distance whom they were fighting against. The mace he carried was designed as per his requirements by the most skilful artisans. Lightweight and streamlined, its heavy but slender silver arm had red rubies studded strategically to ensure a firm grip. A large, rounded, polished, golden hollow solidly crowned the arm, imbued with a sparkling diamond which sported sharp edges on its head. If the enemy was fortunate enough to survive the enormous hit from the mace, he would bleed to death due to the deep gash inflicted by the diamond.

To achieve mastery in wielding weapons, Arjun had to make seemingly impossible sacrifices. He had lived a sheltered childhood. His father, Kartavirya, ensured his son was provided with all the luxuries a prince could ask for. Everything was made available instantly, the minute he clapped his hands. The few times Arjun had moved out of the palace, to break free from the monotony, few of his attendants were fired for not attending to the prince's whims. He envied others who roamed freely on the streets.

Arjun was quite young when his father passed away. As was the custom, Mahismati looked forward to seeing him on the throne, but Arjun had been unaware of the worldly responsibilities of a king. He knew it would be too difficult to shoulder the expectations people had for him.

"To date, it is I who has been cared for by everyone, my entire life. How do you expect me to do it for others?" he asked his father's courtiers.

He gave much thought to what was needed to be done and said, "Consider this my first decision since becoming king; the first decision I ever take for myself. Before I can defend the independence of Mahismati, I must claim it for myself. I renounce the throne which has tied me down all these years. I will return once I believe I deserve it."

Placing the reins of the kingdom in the able hands of Kartavirya's trusted adviser, Arjun set off on his journey. Though his mind was still unclear about what he wanted to achieve from his spiritual quest, Arjun felt a sense of freedom once the palace gates opened to allow him to leave. Giving up the life of luxury would not be hard, he felt. The sage who had visited his father's court when he was a child came to his mind.

"Right now, the only thing I am inheriting from my father is his name.

Kartavirya will be my first name from today," said the proud Arjun. All the kingdoms in the entire *Bharatvarsh* were plagued by feuds for the throne, but Kartavirya Arjun had renounced it so easily. No one in his right mind would throw away something so precious, his subjects thought. Also, no one would get it back so easily once he returned.

"Renounce it once and you have renounced it for life," the commander of the Mahismati army and a good friend of his father had advised him, "There is no greater accomplishment than being a king. Once a true heir gives up his right, the royal relations will besiege it like a pack of hyenas."

Arjun laughed. "I can take it back just as easily as I have given it up. I know what I need to learn to get it back."

Decked in the garb of an ascetic and renouncing all his belongings, Arjun travelled to the desolate lands towards the west where the Narmada merged with the sea. He stayed there for years under austere conditions, learning from renowned *rishis*. The children of other Kshatriya kings who joined the *ashrams* followed a regimental schedule. They were schooled in courses designed to last for, at least, four to twelve years. The teachers divided students based on merit and age, and a designated timetable was prepared where the allotted teachers arrived to begin their lessons, that spanned for a certain number of hours. During the early years, a general curriculum was established for all the students, while the older ones were asked to choose a specialisation like Archery or Mathematics. Periodic tests were conducted to assess the amount of knowledge the students could imbibe during the classes. At the end of the year, before the theories became more complex and intricate, a subject-wise exam was conducted before the students could graduate to a higher grade. But Kartavirya had other plans.

He approached the sages with a request; to teach him everything they knew in a flexible environment. It was difficult to refuse the prince of Mahismati. Arjun requested permission to keep his schedule fluid, where he could decide what he wanted to study, without any mandatory after-class assignments. In return, he promised to provide labour in the *ashram*, like ordinary folk. He volunteered to take classes for students younger than him, to broom and mop the *ashram* floor, and help in the kitchen.

While the other students spent at least eight hours a day learning different subjects, Arjun studied in spurts. He took the classes of his choice while skipping others. His inner zeal pushed him to practice on his own. Sometimes, he could be seen studying near the cowshed - his books open at pages which had not yet been covered in the class, while other times, he spent hours in the training ground shooting arrows. While the other students were seen frantically studying as their exams approached, there was no visible change in Kartavirya's schedule during that time. He excelled at every exam he chose to appear for. Once he felt he had learned everything the sages had to teach him, he moved to the next *ashram*. By the end of that phase in his life, Kartavirya had been a student at almost every popular *ashram* in the central part of the country. His mental and physical acumen was unparalleled, and there was no weapon, invented to date, that he was not adept at handling.

"How did you decide it was time to leave an *ashram* and move on to another? Generally, students appear for tests, but in your case, it was at your behest," Meghraj, the general of the Mahismati army asked once when Arjun had returned.

"Once there's nothing to be jealous of from a sage's storehouse of knowledge," Arjun replied laughingly.

It was only after a decade that Arjun decided to return to his kingdom to claim his throne. By then, he had developed a deep devotion towards Lord Dattatreya, the God with three heads, each representing Brahma, Vishnu and Mahesh, the holy trinity. Like him, Arjun had chosen to wear the saffron robes all his life. Once he returned, he faced no opposition to his legacy, as was feared by his loyal subjects. Arjun's authority was indelibly stamped on the minds of people. His immense knowledge and skill at warfare were unparalleled. For many years, the courtiers had been waiting for the true successor to ascend the throne and reclaim his mantle.

***

A loud knock brought Arjun back to the present. It was still too early to start his day. He unbolted the door with mounting irritation. A prison guard stood before him and quickly kneeled on seeing his king.

"The King of the South refuses to eat anything," the soldier informed him. Mahismati had only one king in their prison. Kartavirya thought for a moment. He usually liked to spend his mornings alone, but this prisoner was quite intriguing. Arjun had grown a liking to his altercations, which had become a routine. Unabashed, unafraid and undaunted - though confined to the four walls - the prisoner's spirit seemed free.

"Since when has he refused to eat?" Arjun asked.

"It's been more than five days now, *Maharaj*," the soldier hesitated while answering his king.

"And you are telling me this now?" Arjun knew what the soldier's reply would be before he heard it.

"We didn't want to bother you with such petty events," the soldier said, with his head bowed. Arjun was tired of hearing this phrase. For a king, it seemed all the happenings in his kingdom were considered petty. It was only when the situation became worse and deemed out of control that he was provided second-hand information. He asked the soldier to wait while he got ready.

The state prison was guarded by a heavy, wrought iron door. It took the strength of at least four, full-grown men to nudge it open. It led to a narrow, seemingly never-ending, badly lit staircase. Anyone descending the stairs would not be able to see where it led to. There was only enough space for one person to descend at a time. There were no other passages through which the prison cells were connected. The whole setup was designed to prevent any prison escapes.

The soldier and the king traversed the foul-smelling, dingy stairs. Arjun never liked being there, but the King of the south had made him walk down that path quite a few times already. There were no isolation chambers in Mahismati. It was only when this king had been captured that Arjun ordered the workers to construct a bigger cell for the occasion. A separate bathroom was attached to his cell. It was built a little further away from other cells, where the common prisoners were kept. The Southern King was known for his powers of persuasion, and Arjun didn't want the other prisoners to come under his influence.

The long period of confinement had taken a toll on the prisoner's body. Though he worked-out regularly, his once muscular sinewy arms had turned frail and thin. His barrel-chest seemed to have lost a few inches. His cheekbones protruded while his eyes seemed to have hollowed out.

However, his personality still carried the dread of yesteryears. There was a certain gloom that seemed to envelop him. It almost seemed like the surroundings were fearful of expressing themselves before him. His face bore deep slashes at various places, and still deeper cuts which ran across his upper torso suggested his experience. He looked like a man with a purpose; one who lived in the future with no concerns about his present. His eyes insinuated he was well-aware of his goals, and that he would refuse to yield before they were seen to; that day was nothing but a single step on his journey towards his goal. The prisoner had never asked for any additional amenities, and survived with what was provided. Years spent in the prison had not affected him physically, but mentally, he was the same king Arjun had faced in one of the most magnificent battles *Bharatvarsh* had witnessed.

Arjun found him sitting in a *yogic* posture in deep meditation, and was informed by the prison guard that the king hasn't moved in days. Meals were being served to him at stipulated hours, only to be removed later.

"Eating this would only do you good," Arjun said, looking at the plate laden with food, untouched.

"Care to join me? Let us eat together, someday," the Brahmin replied calmly, his eyes remaining closed. Arjun had seen many seers lost in contemplation. As an ascetic, he too had practiced the art of meditation. As *rishis* tried to focus their minds on the energy flowing through their bodies, they gauged its interaction with the larger universe, and would dissociate themselves from their immediate external surroundings. With a few years of practice, it became difficult to keep track of changes in the physical conditions outside while meditating. The seers delved into a deep spiritual slumber. Arjun had witnessed many sages lose themselves to the power of concentration, while being physically engulfed in huge storms or heavy rains. But this Brahmin was different. He seemed to be the master of multiple minds; Dashanan – One with ten heads was an apt name for him. While one of his minds tried to concentrate on his energy flowing inwards, the others remained fully aware of the external world. A common soldier couldn't fathom the deep concentration the prisoner was experiencing as he could converse soundly even in that state. Only someone like Arjun, who had performed transcendental meditation a good number of times, could make out how deeply the Brahmin was engrossed.

"I don't dine with criminals," Arjun said in a dismissive tone. His face was flushed as he felt his left cheek twitch.

The Brahmin laughed. He opened his eyes which burned like embers, though his voice maintained the same poise, "It is you who usurped my kingdom and killed my people. Release me, and I will show you what crime means."

The Brahmin had been enraged ever since he was imprisoned. But he had never allowed his anger to get the better of his demeanour. The years of imprisonment hadn't affected his dignity or spirit. He seemed to be channelizing his frustrations internally, letting his insides burn with the humiliation of the defeat. Since his imprisonment, many a time Arjun had insulted the Brahmin, but he never raised his voice.

Arjun ignored his threat. He knew the weight of the war was too heavy on his shoulders.

"I don't think you remember what happened the last time we met. Looking at you right now, I think you would be no more than a sacrificial goat in the duel," Arjun scoffed.

"I remember it as clearly as the waters in the river Narmada. A man must never forget his humiliation. He can choose to forgive the people and the circumstances that led to it, but keep his failures close to his heart. Every day since then, the defeat has gnawed at my heart. In my mind, I have revisited the events at least a thousand times. It had helped me grow as a person. I was filled with foolish pride back then. Like other kings, I was a self-centred megalomaniac who wanted to conquer the whole earth. The wars that I'd waged lacked a reason for people to fight for me. But now, I shall give them a good reason. I will return with twice the vengeance and a chariot-load of venom. Instead of one, you would be facing a pack of proud *Rakshashas*," the half-Brahmin replied calmly.

Arjun stood in silence for a while, trying to understand what the *Rakshasha* King meant. He saw no point in arguing with him since he was stuck with an opinion in his head. He was about to leave when the erstwhile King of Lanka spoke, "Tell me, *Rajan*. Do you envy me?"

Arjun started laughing hysterically; the twitch returned, "What should I be jealous of? You are a broken man who will spend the rest of his life in this dank, smelly prison. Before you stand the wealthiest man, the wisest sage, and the mightiest king. Unlike you, I can achieve whatever I set my eyes on."

Ravan smiled, "Yet, the mightiest king comes down to this dimly-lit cell to talk to this broken man. Your senses are quite shifty, *Rajan*. Be content with what you have. You are already at a place where few have reached."

"You don't need to worry about me. Take care of yourself. The death of the *Rakshasha* King through starvation won't look good," said Arjun, a bit perturbed. It was difficult to hide your emotions from the deciphering mind of the prisoner.

Ravan paused before breaking into a monologue, "Bear with me a little longer, King of Mahismati. I don't bear any hatred in my heart towards you. I have matured since that incident. I have spent my time in this prison reflecting on my past deeds. I fought against you for the sake of pride and arrogance. Had I fought for my people, I would have never lost. I understand it now."

"Fight for the people…," Arjun started laughing hysterically as his voice trailed off. Regaining his composure, he continued, "What people are you talking about? Those who belonged to the same kingdom you forcefully pried from your brother. It seems your solitary time here, in this cell, has played on your senses," he remarked mocking the Brahmin. Very few people had an appetite for such talks so early in the morning.

"Kuber lost to me since he was equally self-obsessed. The throne of Lanka was a mere toy for us. We were selfish kids fighting to satiate our egos. Anyone of us could have won that battle, and it wouldn't have made an iota of difference to the people of Lanka. His greed clashed with my pride and lost against it. But when you fight, not for yourself, but for the people, you understand the utter fragility of your ego. With millions of dreams weighing upon your shoulders, your own becomes insignificant. It is then you fight like no one else can, with the consciousness that your defeat will not only leave you humiliated, but also shatter a million others. You fight till the very end so that the collective dream of your people remains alive," Ravan replied, in all earnestness.

Arjun laughed, "I smell defeat in your words. You cannot change the reality, Ravan. I fought against you and made Lanka my vassal state before everyone's eyes. It is because of my mercy that you are alive now. You won't understand how much I regret it."

"And why do you think you have put me in prison?" the irony rung heavy in Ravan's voice, "Why hasn't Mahismati held any other king as a prisoner? Is it because I am a *Rakshasha*? Because I might defile the Aryan blood if set free?"

Arjun stood in silence as the Brahmin continued. "So much arrogance won't do you any good, Arjun. It seems you are turning into Ravan. Princelings like you have made similar mistakes in the past. They feel entitled to the throne. Such a man draws respect for his position from the people, and not for his character. Such a man is forgotten by the masses as soon as he is ousted."

"There is no king in the *Bharatvarsh* who can defeat me," Arjun said angrily as his hands slipped to his sword, "I will cut anyone to pieces before he can pose a threat to my kingdom."

"Mahismati won't be defeated by weapons. It will only be defeated by spirit and courage. I know, *Rajan,* you are an exceptional warrior, and to fight you in battle is to stand against the Yama himself. But your shortcomings will be the cause of your ruin. Don't bear so much envy in your heart. It will not do you good," intoned Ravan, sounding like he was trying to remember his yesteryears.

Arjun half understood what Ravan meant. His seemingly convoluted arguments were making him angry. He looked to the soldier standing behind him and directed him to take the food plate away. As in the past, he knew the Brahmin won't continue eating for many more days.

"And now, you think you have found this spirit and courage," Arjun said sarcastically.

"Yes, I have. You won't ever win against me now," the Brahmin changed his posture. He now stood on one leg with his arms stretched, and palms pressed against each other over his head.

Arjun smirked, "I think you are quite late."

"This arrogance suits the king of the mightiest kingdom in the entire country. Lanka too had its days of glory," Ravan smiled playfully, his eyes probing Arjun, "Eons ago, I meditated on Lord Brahma, the creator. My father, *rishi* Vishrava had made me well-versed in Vedic learnings and rituals, and I wanted to put it to good use. But Brahma was not an easy God to impress. A lot of sages before me had tried to please him and failed. Months turned into years, but I remained in my *yogic samadhi* waiting for his blessings. It was only after many years that he appeared before me, and asked me for a boon. I still remember how mesmerised I was on seeing him through my mind's eye. The universe had been a small ball of fire in his hands, and one fine day, he'd flicked it, leading to its expansion which hasn't stopped to date. I saw him create all the celestial and non-celestial beings, and later, he passed on the reins of management to Vishnu. Like any mortal, I asked to drink at the fountain of eternal life and youth. The Lord was not impressed. He conveyed that death-life-death is the cycle of nature, and that he wouldn't interfere with it." Arjun was not sure where the conversation was headed. The Brahmin seemed to have lost his mind - talking about watching the creation of the universe so early in the morning!

"Then, I asked him to grant my wish which ensured I couldn't be killed by any God, heavenly spirit, serpent, or wild beast. That boon was readily granted by Lord Brahma, though I skipped mentioning humans. Humans are one of the weakest creations of Brahma. Most of them have weak senses and are unable to figure out where they are headed in life, after which, they die without serving any purpose. Their feeble minds are easily distracted by senseless pleasures and their character remains open to exploitation by debauchery and wickedness. I, Ravan, ignored these feeble creatures. But I regret it now. No matter how weak a creation, each is bestowed with its spark of brilliance. Brahma didn't discriminate amongst his creations. He instilled that spark in everyone, which can be found by anyone who tries hard enough. So, learn from my mistakes, Arjun. Do not underestimate anyone based on his circumstances. You might have to pay dearly for it." Arjun found it difficult to stand the insolence any long. He was used to his stress-free mornings.

"Is someone smuggling intoxicants in here?" Arjun said laughingly, turning towards the soldier accompanying him. "So, you are blessed by Lord Brahma himself. Dashanan - one with ten heads, it seems none of it is in its right place. Here you are, the mighty Brahmin with the blessings of Brahma, cowering for months."

Ravan's laugh ricocheted against the walls of the cell, "Don't you see, Arjun? I am training myself. Training to bring to Lanka the glory it deserves."

"I don't have time for this word jugglery. I would rather hunt than fight a pale Brahmin," Arjun said mockingly before leaving.

"Go for it. Enter the forest and try to meet some wise *rishis*," Ravan's voice followed him.

'Is it because I am a *Rakshasha*?' Ravan's words kept ringing in Arjun's ears as he returned to his palace room. Like Lanka, Mahismati had many vassal states around *Bharatvarsh* who considered Arjun as their leader. Kingdoms like Lanka had been humiliated on the battlefield, but there was no other emperor who had been imprisoned by Mahismati - till now. The defeated kings were re-instated to their thrones with one condition – their foreign policy would be directed towards Mahismati's interest. 'But Lanka was treated differently,' Arjun thought.

***

Arjun tried to remember the events leading to Ravan's capture. Within a few years of his ascension to the throne of Mahismati, Arjun performed the *Ashvamedha yagna* and expanded the boundaries of the Haiyaya kingdom, making it one of the largest empires in *Bharatvarsh*. He fought valiantly against the mighty rulers and quelled their challenge. There was only one emperor who proved to be a formidable opponent in his quest; the new king of the south, the ten-headed demon; Ravan.

Ravan had gained Lanka by defeating his half-brother Kuber. Though small in size, Lanka was the richest amongst all kingdoms. It was strategically positioned at the center of sea trade, which was the backbone of its economy, directed from the mainland. Acting as the resting grounds for the crew, it gained heaps of revenue from taxes, collected from the ships that dropped anchor at the Lankan ports. People in Mahismati referred to it as the city of Gold, the metal which abounded the Lankan treasury. Arjun, known for his desire for all things that glittered, wanted Lanka to become a part of the Haiyaya territory. But Ravan was not one to be subdued easily. Like Arjun, he too was hungry for power. Though his kingdom was separated from the mainland by the sea, he sent several military expeditions to far-off places and bought many powerful kingdoms to their knees against the might of the Lankan army.

Ravan's ten heads represented the fountain of knowledge he had acquired through practice and penance. From what Arjun knew, he was born in a modest *ashram*, a progeny of sage Vishrava and *Rakshashi* Kaikesi. He was home-schooled by his father, but Ravan had quickly surpassed him in his spiritual quest. He then travelled to faraway lands in search of knowledge. He met many sages on his way, but none could contribute new knowledge to the learned Brahmin.

He then placed his trust in the seer of seers, the king of kings, the *adiyogi* Shiva, and decided to take a pilgrimage to his abode, Mount Kailash. Very few mortals had tried to follow the same treacherous path. Most of them met their tragic demise, freezing to death in the crevices of the mountain.

As much as he was stirred by his persistence, Ravan also impressed Shiva with his plenary of talents. He was a quick learner, and never disappointed Shiva in mastering the tricks related to the usage of multiple weapons; be it a sword, mace, or spear. Not only that, Shiva also taught him various military strategies and formations which he knew would assist him as the general of his army. Once his training was complete, Shiva gifted Ravan the Chandrahaas *Khadag*, a sword shaped like the new moon. At the time, no one knew how Ravan would utilise the Chandrahaas, which was believed to possess divine powers.

"Use it wisely," was the only advice Shiva had given him.

The sword designed in the likeness of a pair of lips, which curled into an incongruous smile, rained havoc on the southern peninsula. Ravan and his army of *Rakshashas* captured Lanka and the adjoining territories, and soon, his reputation as a formidable warrior was well established.

"Never believed a *Rakshasha* could perform such a feat," Arjun had heard people say. He too was bemused by Ravan's antics. Not only had he exponentially strengthened Lanka's military, but also worked towards bringing an all-round development and betterment for its citizens.

"A *Rakshasha* has been able to outperform so many Kshatriya kings," many would say, pointing towards the shortcomings of the Mahismati kingdom.

Meanwhile, Arjun's *Ashvamedha yagna* was in progress. As was the tradition, he sent an entourage of unarmed, royal men, with a horse bearing Haiyaya's insignia, to different chiefdoms. The horse symbolized Arjun's suzerainty, and any king who allowed it to enter the city's premises indicated its automatic acceptance, transforming his chiefdom into a vassal state of Mahismati. However, not everyone was prepared for Mahismati to exert its dominance without contention. Many kingdoms, big and small, opposed the leadership of Arjun on their sovereign states. To curb the authority of such states, the soldiers of Mahismati were dispatched, and returned only when the Haiyaya colours were plastered all over the fort walls of the enemy states. The results of the *yagna* were met with far more success than what

Arjun had anticipated. Soon, stories of his conquests became part of the local folklore. His influence extended to nearly the entirety of the central plateau. The soldiers who had fought valiantly for many months sighed with relief on finally being able to rest their weary muscles. Once most of the Kshatriya territory came under the rule of Mahismati, the general of Arjun's army, Meghraj, delightfully implored him to signal the end of the campaign. It had lasted endlessly for the past few years.

"No, Lanka is still left," Arjun huffed with a glint in his eye. The ceaseless war had depleted the treasury of Mahismati, which left the king and his royal courtiers scrambling for ways to replenish it. Lanka was the richest kingdom that Arjun was aware of. It had most of the southern states bordering Mahismati under its command. The king of Mahismati was eyeing the vast amount of gold Lanka had amassed.

"We should leave Ravan alone. We have enough land to proclaim our superiority over all the existing kingdoms of the *Bharatvarsh*," Meghraj shuddered thinking about the devastation the conquest of Lanka might bring.

Even though the expansion of Mahismati had been successful, people were still completely enamoured by Lanka's successes. The discovery of a new trade route, loss of sheen of western ports since the advent of Lanka, a *Rakshasha* king, a learned Brahmin challenging the might of the empires on the mainland, and its copious amount of wealth were the ingredients for an interesting tale. In comparison, Mahismati seemed to undergo a mundane transformation into a power-hungry state.

Arjun wanted to stamp out the Lankan fairy tale from the minds of people. His struggles and triumphs looked tiny in comparison to Lanka. He had overheard many a discussion in his court related to Lanka. 'Without Lanka, the conquest of Mahismati would remain incomplete. It needs what Lanka has; a great story' were his thoughts. Ravan's army was known for the savage treatment of its enemies. Men, women, and children - every citizen of Lanka came forward to protect their lands whenever there was a threat to their kingdom. The Aryan rules of war was lost on them. They were notorious for leaving no survivors while they ceaselessly fought during the day, as at night. Anyone rendered unarmed was killed ruthlessly. Some of the soldiers who dithered from raising weapons at the Lankan women knew they'd committed a horrible mistake since the women were as merciless as the men. Light on their feet, they fought against men and beasts twice their size with ease.

"They are weary from the last war," Arjun remarked, referring to the recent sea attack launched by Lanka on the islands towards the west. He knew his counterpart, Ravan, was an equally ambitious king. "Also, it is difficult for them to manage their assets on the mainland being surrounded by the sea on all sides. I think the dummy *Rakshasha* kings installed by Ravan would yield without much opposition. After all, the news of our numerous conquests must have reached them."

'Are they as weary as we are?' Meghraj thought. He remained sceptical of Arjun's plans. "They have fought countless wars. I think they wait for it to happen. I have seen his brethren fight. They seem to be most alive in battle. Forcing Ravan to toe the line would be difficult. All the kings he has installed in his territory are fiercely loyal to him and ensure their master's commands are carried out."

Arjun chose to ignore his general's views. "You cannot live fearlessly and prosper if your neighbour is equally strong. Mahismati needs weak neighbours across its borders." Arjun asked the general to pick a few of the most courageous men from his army. The head priest was asked to prepare the sacrificial horse, along with an entourage of unarmed ambassadors, for the last leg of its journey to the territory of Ravan. The ambassadors, though loyal to the king, asked him to reconsider his decision. *Rakshashas* were not known to be kind to people who brought bad news to them.

"This will be the last time I am sending you to the enemy's kingdom. The *Ashvamedha yagna* will end once Lanka kneels before me," Arjun commanded, bidding farewell to the entourage.

"Look at this before you leave," the king's voice boomed behind his soldiers who had started their journey. Arjun's face twitched as he held a gold coin glittering in his palm against the sun, "This will be our prize for winning. No other kingdom is as wealthy as Lanka. The citizens of Mahismati will have more riches than they can dream of."

Khara had been crowned the king of Dandaka, and it was there that the entourage of Arjun was headed. A few months prior, he had informed Ravan regarding the *Ashvamedha* sacrifice being conducted by Arjun.

"Let the king conquer as many territories as he wants to, as long as he doesn't threaten Lanka. Gouge his eyes out if that ever happens. We cannot compromise on any portion of our motherland," the return letter from Ravan stated.

Khara had increased vigil at Dandaka borders following that. The *Rakshashas* guarded their kingdom's boundaries by thick jungles; surroundings that highly suited their combat skills. They were experts at deploying guerrilla tactics against any mighty army. It made the neighbouring kings think twice before entering those regions. It was through these thickets that the fearful men of Mahismati's entourage entered Lankan territory on foot, unarmed, with the decorated horse silently in tow.

Dusk was breaking when they set foot inside Lanka's boundary. There was not one single visible road in front of them that led anywhere.

"We could get lost if we continue on our journey during the night. Let us wait for the sun to rise again," one of the entourage opinionated. The ambassadors heeded the advice of their fellow traveller. As per their knowledge, the city boundaries of Dandaka *van* was still quite a distance away, and it would take at least three to four more days to reach there. They soon discovered a stretch with a less dense undergrowth, and cleared it using the crude tools they carried with them. Tying the horse to a tree, they laid their gear on the ground and prepared to camp for the night.

It was close to midnight when the group decided to retire. The entire day had been spent on travelling and their aching feet needed rest. A deer killed during the day was cooked for the night's dinner. Though a few stayed wide awake; unable to fall asleep after the heavy meal. Falling asleep in Rakshasha territory was a nightmare for them.

The forest was unusually silent that night. Manvendra, a burly man who was sleeping at one end of the group, had been tossing and turning for hours. Every time he tried closing his eyes, trepidations over his violent death at the hands of demons consumed his mind. He looked towards his fellowmen who were sleeping next to him in a neat row. Covered by a white sheet to block the cold, they resembled corpse placed next to each other. Manvendra shifted to his left to block the image of himself lying next to the faux dead bodies. The narrow clearing which served as their camping grounds was surrounded by thick hardwood trees that had stood on the earth for hundreds of years. The group had tied a few lit torches to the trees to keep animals at bay. Against the light from the torches, he noticed the eerie sheen of the white horse. It was tied at a safe distance from them. The animal, too, seemed tired from the long journey. Manvendra had seen it fall asleep many a time whilst it stood in place. It was a phenomenon unique to this species. Horses, known for their speed, had evolved to be able to sleep without having to lie down and locking their knees. It helped save time if they were ever attacked by a predator. But that day, it seemed like the animal had decided to let its guard down.

The torches near the horse burned bright, gently illuminating the night. The group had placed at least four torches around the animal. It was the most valuable item they possessed, and they wanted its surroundings to remain well lit. Manvendra eyes darted from one torch to another. His senses seemed unaffected by the long travel. Suddenly, he saw a small flicker at a distance, just behind the horse. The thick vegetation and bright light emanating from the torches blinded Manvendra's vision. He was unable to make out anything in the dark. He thought about waking his colleagues up, but their snoring reminded him of how tired they all were. He laid down, still praying that the flame would move away from the group, but instead, it kept growing bigger and brighter in the distance. He tried to get his eyes to adjust to the darkness, focusing at a spot away from the torchlight. To his surprise, a second flame accompanied the first, which was soon followed by another. The entourage was being raided by the *Rakshashas*. A loud cry escaped Manvendra's throat causing everyone around him, including the horse, to awaken, but it was too late. The whole group was surrounded by the malevolent *Rakshashas* from all sides by then.

"Where are you from?" one of the *Rakshashas* growled at them.

"We are ambassadors of King Kartavirya Arjun. You might know him as Sahastrarjun; one with the thousand arms. We have come here to meet your King Khara," Manvendra said shaking in his shoes.

A burst of cumulative laughter was the response he received. He looked around. The huge, mighty *Rakshashas* were closing in.

"We are unarmed and have not entered your territory with any intention of harming anyone," someone from Manvendra's group cried out. The tremble in his voice was evident.

"That makes it easier for us," one of the *Rakshashas* said stretching his arms. He picked up one of the men from the group by the neck, his grip tightening as the others looked on in abject horror. Manvendra's eyes moved frantically around. Soon, every one of his colleagues, including him, found themselves with their feet in the air. Manvendra was frothing at his mouth. He lost consciousness soon, but not before seeing the many sharp blades slicing the *Ashvamedha* horse.

As foretold by his advisors, Arjun understood that Lanka wouldn't yield easily. In a few days, a few fishermen visited his court. The whereabouts of the *Ashvamedha* horse and the Mahismati entourage were still unknown. Arjun had received no official message or warning from the court of Khara. The *Rakshasha* king hadn't bothered to convey his discomfort to Mahismati regarding their expansion plan. The fishermen had discovered several severed body parts bearing Haiyaya colours in the adjoining sea. Arjun smiled widely when the fishermen opened the casket carrying the remains of his soldiers. In the end, he had found a worthy opponent.

"Courage, pride, wealth – I will crush everything this *Rakshasha* holds." Meghraj could see the muscles on his king's face tremble.

***

"Lanka is too far away. Our soldiers will die of starvation before reaching that place," Meghraj raised his concerns. He was afraid the king's greed would throw the whole empire into a fight which might prove to be too costly.

"We won't reach Lanka by land," Arjun said laughing menacingly. Expeditions through sea were unheard of. It would require, not only loading the soldiers onto ships, but also the chariots, elephants, horses, armour, and weapons. Food supplies, medicines, and clothing which were vital for the soldiers to survive the many weeks of their upcoming journey were also needed. While the battle would cost many lives, the general was afraid that seasickness and other diseases might eat away at many of his soldiers.

"We need to go back to the drawing board to discuss the modalities. I am sure this is going to cost us a fortune," the head treasurer of Mahismati echoed his general's views.

"And you think I am not aware of it?" Arjun scoffed, "Don't worry. We will gain more than our fill from Lanka's conquest to fuel many such future expeditions. Besides, I want to witness the courage of its king at close quarters. Despite knowing those were Mahismati's soldiers, the strongest of all kingdoms, he didn't think twice about murdering them." The tinker of gold rung heavily in Arjun's ears. The loss of his loyal ambassadors hadn't affected his views about the conquest of Lanka even the slightest.

"Your wish is our command," the head priest intoned as Arjun dismissed his council. None of them seemed supportive of his decision. 'Nevertheless, they will follow me,' Arjun bemused, a luxury reserved for kings.

Soon, architects, designers, carpenters, and other workmen started gathering at the ports of Mahismati. As per the king's order, they busied themselves with building ships bigger than anything anyone had ever seen. Softwood was imported from far-off lands and ambitious designs were presented before the king's council waiting for approval. The construction started in full swing at Mahismati's harbours which quickly turned into a pilgrimage ground of sorts. The citizens began frequenting the place, completely awestruck by the limitlessness of human imagination.

"Do you think such large ships could sail on the ocean? What keeps them afloat, if not the blessings of the sea god?" people could be heard asking each other.

It took close to six months to complete the construction of the fleet. The council, though reluctant, remained faithful to its king and toiled tirelessly to ensure his plans emerged successfully. Though they had their doubts about the expedition, it didn't dither them from their duties.

"We should not forget our history, Arjun. No other king has sent so large an army overseas," warned the head priest as the construction of the ships was nearing its end.

"And that is why we will win," laughed Arjun triumphantly, dismissing the priest's apprehensions.

"We need to build more ships," Arjun turned towards his general, "Lanka is just the start. The boundaries of the kingdom of Mahismati should stretch till the ends of the earth." The general nodded hesitatingly. He knew his opinions would fall on deaf ears.

"Why are you so hell-bent on conquering Lanka?" the head priest asked Arjun.

"Because it has more gold than you can imagine," Arjun said, his right-hand tinkering with the gold coins in his pocket.

"A lot of people cannot imagine the amount of gold Mahismati has in its stores," the head priest argued.

"I want what Ravan has. A perennial supply of gold coins because of the Lankan ports," said Arjun.

"You have enough wealth for many generations to come. Don't be envious of what others possess, son," the priest persisted, imploring the king to give up his zealous ideas of military campaign.

"Had I not been envious of others, I would have never been able to wear these saffron robes," Arjun laughed, "the *Ashvamedha* horse would still be standing in its inn. Mahismati is far from being on the same level as Lanka, but I will snatch everything from Ravan."

Finally, the day arrived when they had to bid farewell to their motherland. The ships were docked majestically at the port, waiting for the travellers to embark on their journey. A handsome, white horse was anointed by the high priests and loaded onto the ship. The treasurer, along with the other courtiers of Mahismati, looked on with increasing worry at the proceedings. For months now, he had been busy estimating the costs involved.

"In a few weeks, you would be thanking me for undertaking this risk," said Arjun looking towards his courtiers. A silent prayer escaped the treasurer's lips, 'Hope the king's words come true.'

"I am not sure whom the king is more jealous of – Lanka, or his own subjects," the priest whispered into the treasurer's ears.

The journey to Lanka remained uneventful. Though a few soldiers and animals experienced bouts of seasickness, there were no major incidents that worried Meghraj. Within a few days, the ships reached the Lankan coast. The shores looked blissfully serene, devoid of any visible risk. The *Rakshashas*, it seemed, didn't have an inkling of their arrival. The soldiers were worn out from their long travel, but nonetheless, prepared themselves for the treacherous battle ahead. It was only their king's exuberance that hadn't been affected by this long arduous journey. He seemed to be eagerly waiting for the enemy to arrive.

"It seems we have won half the battle," Arjun was happy that the knowledge of his attack hadn't reached the *Rakshasha* king. Meghraj nodded, half-believing the empty shores to be a trap.

The Haiyaya army anchored and de-boarded the ships. As anticipated by their general, they didn't have to wait very long for the enemy to arrive. The local fishermen who had been watching their movements for many hours had rushed towards the capital to inform Ravan.

"Everyone seems to be working for money," Ravan's voice reverberated throughout the walls of the palace. He was seething with anger. "Has the loyalty to your clan escaped your blood?" his question was directed towards Vibhishan.

"We are warring at multiple fronts. After Khara killed their entourage, we had sent a Lankan battalion to his kingdom. We had assumed that Arjun would be attacking through the land," Vibhishan said politely with his head bowed. He too was disappointed by the inefficiency of the Lankan detectives.

Since assuming the throne of Lanka, Ravan felt he had been unusually hard on his brother. Under Vibhishan's leadership, the army of Lanka had conquered many territories and brought them under its control. While the lapse was significant, Ravan decided to ignore it.

"I had promised to lead our army in the battle against Mahismati. Come, my brother, let us do it together. Let us show Arjun the mettle of our *Rakshasha* clan," Ravan patted Vibhishan's shoulder. "Let this battle be remembered for ages. While the Haiyaya army may have reached Lanka, let us make sure that they are not able to return."

Ravan reached the parapet on the roof and looked towards the western shores. Taking his position behind the large drums, he began beating them incessantly. The drums were sounded whenever the population of Lanka needed to be alerted. The battle was about to begin.

The Lankan seas turned red. Sea creatures feasted as human flesh and blood choked the shores. The swollen bodies of soldiers, covered in different colours, lay rotting on the shores. Elephants and horses, maimed and injured, roamed among the dead. Vibhishan saw, from a distance, a murder of crows pecking on the insides of a horse that was still very much alive, but was unable to move. The bodies of the dead covered the entire shore, stretching out as far as the eye could see. But there seemed to be no end to this tragedy.

The ravaging army of Lanka, though vicious in their attacks, were untrained in comparison to their enemies. Battle formations and military strategies were lost on them. Not many years ago, they had been farmers who tilled their lands. But their cruelty knew no bounds. Devoid of fear, they moved in hordes against the disciplined battalions of Mahismati. It didn't matter what battle formation Meghraj followed because, by the end of the day, the Lankan army had marauded their camps while losing thousands of their brethren. Neither side could see an end to this war, but both the kings refused to give up.

"We need to stop this bloodshed, Ravan," said Vibhishan, "It is doing more harm than good." The agony was etched on his face. It has been more than a week since the war had started. Lanka had lost many of its brave soldiers. Those alive stared with blank expressions at their general. Each one felt they were next in line to be killed by the army of Mahismati.

"Not before I have drawn the blood of Kartavirya Arjun. He dared to challenge the *Rakshashas*. I will make sure his armour and chariot don't leave the shores of Lanka," Ravan roared. Death danced to his tunes at the Haiyaya camp.

"Bring forth your king. I shall make him meet his maker," Ravan bellowed with bloodshot eyes. None of the brave warriors of the Haiyaya army were strong enough to challenge his might. The Chandrahaas had been busy drawing the blood of the enemies.

"Wish we had some warriors on our side with similar courage. We need to find a way to stamp out this king of Lanka. I hadn't presumed to meet him on the battlefield. His ferociousness is contagious and makes his soldiers fight with more abandon," Arjun too was smitten by Ravan's spirit.

"He penetrates through any formation I try. Be it *Garud, Makar,* or *Trishul Vyuha,* nothing works against him. Yesterday, we tried to trap him using *Chakra Vyuha*. Ravan broke through the bait easily, the light infantry placed at the front, to enter the *Vyuha*. By giving him obstacles that were not too difficult to subdue, we bought him to the centre of the spiral in no time. We didn't leave an inch for him to escape. The best of Mahismati's warriors were unleashed who surrounded him. Supported by elephants and the cavalry, it seemed like the war was finally coming to an end. But nothing seems to deter the *Rakshasha* king. He chose a direction for himself and kept moving forward. Whipping and slashing through the formation, he killed anyone and everyone in his sights. By the end of the day, we had lost a few of our most gifted generals and the *Vyuha* was in tatters," Meghraj said complementing his king's thoughts.

"Think about the number of deaths in our camp. There must be some way to end this war," Vibhishan opinionated, looking around the battlefield with worry. Both sides were exhausted with fighting day in and day out.

"You are the wisest among us, brother. Let me know a way out of it," Ravan riveted his eyes towards his brother, "Until you come up with such a plan, let me send a few more soldiers of Mahismati to the embrace of death." It has been many years since Ravan had fought a war. But that hadn't dampened his abilities. He was fighting with the same fearlessness and vigour he was known for.

The next day, the weary armies of Mahismati and Lanka stood against each other again. Decrepit and spent from the nonstop fighting that had dragged on for days, both armies wanted the ordeal to end soon. Their fearful eyes were fixated towards the sea which had turned a deep shade of crimson. The blood of the friends and families churned together with that of the enemies.

"Let us keep fighting for our motherland. There is no better way to die," the voice of Meghraj rose above the sound of the sea waves.

But the soldiers were not too sure by then. The ever-expanding realm of their motherland had caused conflict in their minds about what it constituted. They wanted to return to their homes and live peacefully, far away from the dangers of the bloodthirsty *Rakshashas*.

There was still some time left before dawn; the stipulated moment for the battle to start. Ravan's eyes were fixed towards the eastern horizon, waiting for the sun to rise. Both parties waited with bated breaths. Once the war commenced, the soldiers fought until the wee hours of the night. Ravan had realized his armies needed rest to recuperate. He also wanted time to strategize his battle plans. The Mahismati army was agile and trained, which made it difficult to break through their ranks.

"We can decide the result through a trial by combat," Vibhishan suggested as he pulled his chariot near Ravan.

Ravan looked at him quizzically. It took him a few moments to register what Vibhishan was referring to.

"We can send Kumbhkarn and let the Haiyaya ruler choose a fighter from their side," continued Vibhishan.

Kumbhkarn was one of the mightiest warriors on the Lanka's side. Neither of the brothers had ever witnessed someone as powerful as him in close combat. His enormous girth never interfered with his agility. Over the past few days, he had been wreaking havoc in the Haiyaya camp.

Ravan contemplated for a moment. He could see how both sides possessed almost equal strength and were able to cause adequate damages to the other. While he might be able to defeat the army of Haiyaya, the loss taken by the military might would take years to salvage. Sending Kumbhkarn for a duel might bring an abrupt end to the war which was eating into Lanka's finances.

"Would Arjun accept the proposal?" he asked.

"There is no harm in asking," Ravan nodded to Vibhishan's assertion, "It is our best bet. The Haiyaya army is still unaware of our brother's prowess."

Vibhishan asked his army to raise the white flag for the Haiyaya camp to see. He raced his chariot towards the enemy formation.

"Be careful," he heard Ravan's voice from behind.

Vibhishan smiled. He had nothing to worry about while fighting against an army that followed the Aryan rules of war to the hilt. Arjun saw the general from the opposite side approach his camp and asked his soldiers to lower their arms. Halting his chariot near the Haiyaya general, Vibhishan conveyed the message to him.

"Are you sure you have consulted with Ravan?" Meghraj asked. He couldn't believe his ears. The bloodthirsty Ravan was looking to end the treacherous battle.

Vibhishan laughed. He was aware of his brother's reputation. "Consider this a direct proposal from the king of Lanka," he said.

"The king is asking for the ambassador of Lanka to be brought to him," Meghraj's train of thoughts was broken by a soldier at his side. The general nodded and directed his chariot towards Arjun, while trying to identify the strongest men on his side.

Arjun listened intently to what the Lankan general had to say. "So many days of fighting has fatigued the Lankan army. It seems you are unsure if you will be able to overcome us," he mocked.

"Yes, as unsure as you are," Vibhishan was unflinching, "The King and I believe this is the only way both sides could avoid more bloodshed. Your soldiers are as exhausted as mine, and it is the only humane way to escape this quandary we have forced ourselves into."

"You are right, general. Too much blood has been shed on this soil. Ask your king to send his ableist warrior because it will be the ruler of the Haiyaya kingdom who will be fighting from our side," Arjun said, removing his armour.

"But, Arjun, there are many of us who would happily give our lives for Mahismati. Your life is too valuable to be risked," Meghraj was not convinced.

"Who is better than I, in the Haiyaya army?" Arjun snapped at his general.

Arjun's anger dissipated as soon as he saw his general retreat from the argument. In a gentler tone, he continued, "It is important that we win this battle. Not only for Mahismati, winning it would constitute *Aryavarta's* answer to the scourge of *Rakshashas*," Vibhishan tried to ignore Arjun's insinuations, "and we would dither from our duty towards our motherland if we do not send the strongest warrior from our side. It is merely a coincidence that, in this case, it is the king of Mahismati who fulfils the requirements."

Arjun looked towards Vibhishan who gave a respectful bow and asked his charioteer to return. He had never heard of an instance where the king himself chose to fight. He felt a tinge of respect in his heart for the enemy.

"Let us see if your king possesses the same courage," he heard Arjun's voice as he was headed back to the Lankan army.

"Don't be foolish, Ravan. Arjun fighting for his side means nothing. You know Kumbhkarn is an expert in wrestling. Arjun has underestimated our strength. Let us take advantage of it," Vibhishan tried to convince Ravan. Once his elder brother heard Mahismati's decision, he too decided to fight in the duel.

"Do you think I would lose?" Ravan asked empathetically. His nostrils flared on seeing the doubt clouding Vibhishan's face.

"Wars are not won through emotions. We should be driven by what the circumstances have to offer. We have Dushana and Kumbhkarn in our army. In their presence, it doesn't make sense for you to fight,"

Vibhishan's pleas fell on deaf ears.

"It would be an insult to my family if I chose not to fight. Don't you see, brother? The king of Mahismati has challenged our pride," Ravan was seething with anger.

From his experience, Vibhishan knew his prodding won't have much effect on Ravan. He looked around at the Lankan army and its able warriors. Everyone looked towards them for a sound decision.

He tried to sound enthusiastic, "May you have the blessings of Shiva. Show Arjun the kind of courage Lanka holds in its heart."

Arjun asked his charioteer to take him to the centre of the battlefield where Ravan stood. His golden chariot stood majestically against the black carrier of Ravan. Taking control of the reins, Arjun whipped his horses into a frenzy and had them speeding head-on towards Ravan. Ravan stood calmly watching his enemy's movement. He had heard a lot about Arjun's chariot and wanted to see what it could do. He started towards Arjun, coaxing his horses gently. The enemy was just a few metres away at that point. Ravan was prepared to absorb the hit, but at the last second, Arjun swerved to the left. Shiny, pointed spears were pushed out from the periphery of his chariot's wheels, which kept growing in length. Ravan tried to deflect them but it was too late.

The spears cut through a couple of horses tied to Ravan's chariot, which broke into smithereens. The Lankan king landed on the ground with a loud thud. Before he could realise what was happening, a heavy mace started pounding him, trying to bury him into the ground. Ravan caught it mid-air, but a slash across his back dealt by Arjun's sword made him lose his grip. Arjun aimed the diamond embedded in the crown of the mace onto the fresh wound. He tried to ram it in as deep as possible. Crying in pain, Ravan bolted from Arjun's wrath. He balanced himself on his feet, his body visibly trembling due to the beating he'd taken and drew out an *urumi* sword. Extremely sharp, yet lightweight, the *urumi* consisted of multiple long and flexible sword blades which could be used as a whip. Swinging it over his head, Ravan directed it towards Arjun. Multiple blades slashed through Arjun's body. Before he could react, Ravan's dexterous grip had lashed at his other side. Arjun knew the long *urumi* sword can only be resisted by moving closer to the enemy. He tried using the mace to defend himself. The mace got entangled around the blades of the *urumi*. Ravan pulled at the sword with as much force as he could muster. The weapons disengaged themselves from the warriors and went flying. Arjun was able to close the distance between them. Ravan noticed Arjun charging towards him like an enraged bull. The *Rakshasha* king was looking for this opening. Hidden under his knuckles with a horizontal handgrip was an easy to conceal *katar* of diminutive size. As Arjun moved closer, Ravan used it to puncture his armour at multiple places, drawing blood from each of his wounds. Laughing maniacally, he shredded the golden armour of the king of Mahismati and rendered it useless. Using his free hand, he strangled Arjun while persisting with the usage of *katar* to slow his enemy down. Arjun knew time was slipping from his hands. He concentrated on the wound on Ravan's back. He pushed his long sword into the gash and forced it deeper into the exposed flesh. Whilst holding Ravan in a tight embrace, he tried to rip open the skin around the wound using his free hand. The Lankan army shuddered on hearing its king writhing in agony. Arjun's fingers, along with his sword, were now deep inside the wound. He could feel Ravan's grip around his neck loosen. The *katar* fell from Ravan's hands. Arjun twisted his sword inside Ravan's body. Soon, the king of Lanka lost consciousness and was down on the ground, only to awaken in the prison of Mahismati. Years spent on the banks of the

Narmada hadn't been in vain for Arjun.

"Lanka has been conquered and Vibhishan is the new king," Arjun said as Ravan lay in his prison cell, examining his bandaged body.

"Why did you bring me here?" Ravan said looking at the dingy prison cell.

"Don't you remember being defeated miserably while fighting me?" taunted Arjun, laughing at his face.

"Am I the first you have defeated in a battlefield?" Ravan asked. Arjun huffed and left the *Rakshasha* king alone with his miseries.

Ravan sat for hours, trying to remember the chain of events. He saw himself being mauled by Arjun's mace as his army stood laughing menacingly at his plight. He saw Vibhishan handing over the flag of Lanka to Arjun and the general of Mahismati passing the reins of the *Ashvamedha* horse to him. He saw Vibhishan pleading with Arjun, asking to set him free and be taken to the hospital while the Mahismati general chained the Lankan king. He saw Arjun hurl insults at the army of Lanka right before its general.

"A *Rakshasha* is not fit to rule by himself. Consider it his fortune that he will be allowed into the prisons of one of the strongest kingdoms of the *Aryavarta*," Arjun roared.

"No other king had been imprisoned by Mahismati," cried Vibhishan.

"This is our first encounter with a *Rakshasha*, and we want it to be last. You belong in the jungle. Don't you dare try to build any cities," Arjun spat on the ground.

He looked angrily towards the Lankan army; their heads hung in shame. The army of Mahismati, on the other hand, was celebrating their victory over Lanka.

"King Vibhishan," Arjun said patting his shoulders, "Open the palace gates. We want to see what riches the kingdom of Lanka holds for us."

Arjun still remembered how he and his soldiers had entered the premises of Lanka and were bedazzled by the treasures there. Even the houses of the common people held enough gold and ornaments inside. The soldiers of Mahismati were free to steal any amount of gold they wanted. The old, adults, and children watched helplessly as the Mahismati soldiers pillaged their households. They looked for metal hidden in containers holding grains. They tore open mattresses to find hidden jewels. They broke open the locked, wooden almirahs and tore through the pages of books. Arjun made his way to the Lankan palace as his soldiers were busy rummaging through the belongings of the locals. He headed straight towards the treasury and was not disappointed.

"We will leave the animals here," Arjun said referring to the horses and elephants his army had brought with them. "Make sure the Haiyaya ships do not leave the Lankan shores till they are filled to the brim," he directed Vibhishan looking at the treasury.

The wealth of Lanka was loaded onto the Mahismati's ships and within a day, they were ready to sail back to the mainland.

"I think we have enough to survive for generations. What is it that you possess now?" Arjun sneered at Ravan.

Ravan looked at Arjun and smiled, "My pride, which brought about my downfall. Your envy will bring yours."

But that was a thing of the past. Lanka stood vanquished, ruled by Vibhishan who paid handsomely to the king to fill Mahismati's coffers every month. The expedition of Lanka had been the most profitable one for the king.

Arjun looked around his room. His walls were decorated with the stuffed heads of ferocious, wild animals. The early morning confrontation with Ravan had awakened his senses. He decided to follow his suggestion. Mahismati's emperor was known for frequenting the jungle to collect trophies to adorn his walls. 'It's been many months now,' Arjun thought. He called for his attendant to prepare his mount for a wild game.

<u>PARSHU</u>

Four years had passed since the chubby kid had transformed into a full-grown, muscular man. He spent every single day rigorously training, ever since he had reached his master's abode. Come rain, storm, or snow, the student made it a point to not miss even a single day of practice. Like his master, he had achieved immense control over his senses. His body soon got acclimatized to the frugal life on one of the most treacherous environments on earth. A certain calmness had descended over him in those few years. The frown had become less visible. It was only his eyes that remained as cold as mount Kailash, but turned fiery red while facing an enemy.

"Don't let your anger dissipate. Let it flow through your veins. Let it burn through your insides. Let it swallow you whole. Channel it and wield it against any obstacle you face. Let it be a power to you, rather than for others," his master used to say.

But it was easier said than done. Ram was quick to temper. Shiva had seen him struggle with it many a time at the beginning of his training.

"Your wrath is your greatest weakness. It makes you commit mistakes. Your talent won't save you unless you are able to master it," Shiva himself was known for his anger, but his sanguine state was popular as Bholenath - one who can be easily pleased. "Wrath, pride, envy, greed, gluttony, sloth, and lust – these are the seven sins men should guard against. They will be his greatest strengths if they internalise it but can quickly turn into weaknesses. I look for students who show an excess of any of these qualities. My task is to temper them and help them realise their true potential," Shiva said.

Ram knew Shiva was quite selective of his students. "Have you failed at any point?" he asked.

Shiva sighed deeply. "Once," he said, his eyes looking into the void. "And I don't want to fail again," he raised his voice in mock anger, "You need to learn to control your temper quickly. Let it not define you."

Shiva was immensely pleased by Ram's progress. His hunch hadn't betrayed him. The child from Malana was indeed special. In a year's time, he had learned to fight like his father, but it was not enough; there was a hunger for more. He tried his hand at every weapon and excelled in all of them. Kailash had limited means to simulate real-life situations. Hence, every two months or so, the duo travelled to nearby jungles in search of a target; wild beasts, *Rakshashas*, or demons, and till then, the child hadn't missed one. With four years of training coming to an end, the master had decided to hand him his choicest weapons.

The teacher stood up and went to his cave. He opened a large closet lying in a corner, the size of which could hold arms for an entire battalion. The layers of dust settled on top suggested it was seldom used. The wooden lid creaked as it was opened, revealing the plethora of weapons it held. Spears, maces, knives – the box contained weapons of all shapes and sizes. His hands reached for a bow lying on the side. The three-stringed bow was much larger in size and looked quite sturdy. His hands caressed it softly as he tried to remember its past. It had remained his companion in a lot of battles. He had crafted the bow with his own hands. Using Kalpavriksha's wood, he had worked for months to create a bow that would befit only the divine.

Only a few who were worthy had been the recipients of such weapons in the past. Built using ancient wood and sacred rocks, these weapons held the very essence of creation and the mantra of its destruction. They imbued extreme power to their owners. Only a man worthy of such weapons could wield them.

He didn't wish for their powers to be abused like the previous weapon he had gifted to his favourite student. Impressed by the devotion and perseverance of his last disciple, he'd gifted him a sword; the Chandrahaas *Khadag*, but he had been betrayed. Ravan had been an exceptional student, a scholar without equal. Shiva was quickly impressed by his devotion, and in return, gave him the mother of all swords. But he was not happy with how his blessing turned out to be a curse for innocent people. His sword sliced through men and women of all ages without discrimination. Countless lives had been sacrificed at Lanka's altar and the whole country oozed blood owing to the indiscriminate use of Chandrahaas. Most of the kings had given up their thrones to protect their subjects from the utter havoc Ravan had bought to their doorsteps, while others surrendered to their greed in finding an ally who could cast fear in the hearts of even the strongest men.

'One bad experience doesn't mean you should give up on your beliefs. Even Ravan needs to look inside himself,' he thought, running his fingers across the bow. The teacher believed in the basic goodness of all creations. He was about to return to his student when his eyes were riveted to a box that had not been opened in the last few decades. He tried to remember the purpose for which it had been opened last, but the reason completely eluded his mind. He contemplated handing over that weapon as well. It was as powerful as the Chandrahaas - if not more.

Shiva pushed the top lid open. The rusted hinges groaned and fell apart. The heavy lid fell on the ground with a loud thud. Inside was a long-armed gleaming axe. The handle was etched with imprints of human flesh suggesting its heavy usage. The metal gleamed even after being used indiscriminately.

Shiva picked up the axe and the bow and went outside. Ram had just finished his morning workout and was preparing to go for a bath. He saw his master approaching him with weapons of designs he hadn't seen or could have imagined, till then. The weapons majestically decorated with intricate carvings, sized bigger than their counterparts, gleamed brilliantly under the sun.

"Your days at Kailash end today, except for one last test," Ram was startled by his teacher's words, unsure of how to react. He had an inkling that his training was coming to an end, but the announcement sounded too abrupt. He waited in deference to hear whether his teacher had anything else to say.

Placing the bow on the ground, Shiva handed him the axe. Ram still didn't understand what he was supposed to do with it. Shiva picked up his trident which was lying beside a mount and used its rear end to hit Ram squarely on his chest. Ram lost his balance and shuffled back a few feet.

"Fight me," Shiva said, pointing the sharp antlers of his trident towards Ram.

Ram stood glued to his place. Never in his dreams had he imagined raising arms against Shiva, the lord of destruction. Shiva gave him another nudge using the sharp edge of the trident. Ram whimpered in pain but stood his ground while clutching his axe.

"Don't worry, I will stop the fight before one of us kills the other," Shiva said and pushed the trident hard just below his right shoulder. A streak of blood escaped Ram's body. The frown on his forehead grew deeper. He struck the trident heavily with his axe, gazing angrily into Shiva's eyes. Shiva assumed his fighting stance against Ram, with the trident pointed to his heart, and invited Ram to challenge him.

Taking a few steps back, Ram flew towards his teacher. The axe and the trident were locked mid-air, and with one enormous pull, Shiva yanked the axe from Ram's grip which flew a few metres away before landing on the ground.

"Put your heart into this fight. Prove to me that you are a worthy student," Shiva locked Ram's muscular arm between the trident's antlers and started twisting it, slowly pinning him down with his legs over his chest. Ram's cry of pain echoed throughout the snow-clad peaks surrounding them. Though he held immense respect for his teacher, he felt his blood boil. He had performed exceptionally well in all the tests he had to face, but his patience was running thin against this last, and perhaps, most difficult hurdle. He tried to remove his arm from the lock but failed. Hot tears of frustration welled up in the corners of his eyes. He looked to his teacher who smiled maniacally at him; his dreadlocks covering half his face. It felt like his arm was about to break. Finally, using every bit of strength he could muster, he catapulted himself into the air using the lock as a fulcrum and landed on his feet before launching a kick midair to Shiva's abdomen. Both the warriors were flung in opposite directions due to the force of his kick and landed heavily on the ground.

Shiva smiled. Taking the fallen axe from the ground, he flung it towards Ram. "Fight," he commanded.

With a roar, Ram charged towards his teacher. It was time to show his master the outcome of his training. Once he had closed the distance between them to a few feet, the short, muscular Ram flung himself into the air with his axe held above his head. But Shiva was quick to dodge. He moved swiftly, leaving Ram to slash through the empty air and land on the empty ground. Shiva locked his trident against Ram's axe and flung it away from him. With his opponent unarmed, he aimed his trident at Ram's legs.

A searing pain shot through Ram's thigh at the impact. Shiva was pushing the trident against his muscles as hard as he could, showing no mercy to his student. Ram looked to his teacher with pleading eyes, but Shiva refused to budge. The trident had nearly reached the bones of Ram. Ram stretched his arm to the fullest trying to reach for his axe lying on the ground, but Shiva had him firmly fixed to the spot.

Unable to reach his axe while Shiva pinned him down, Ram took hold of Shiva's trident and tried to pull it out of his flesh. But the lord of destruction was not one to give up easily. He kept pushing the trident with all his might while Ram used all his strength to push it away. Though Shiva had him pinned down forcefully, a few seconds later, the trident began moving away from Ram's thighs. Shiva was pleasantly surprised seeing Ram pushing against his strength. Still on the ground, Ram aimed for Shiva's legs and kicked him hard at his shin. Shiva fell, face first, onto the ground, which gave Ram enough time to pick his axe.

A rhythmic dance descended on Mount Kailash with the periodic twang of weapons reverberating through the sky. The master and his student kept their frenzied pace going, testing their strengths against each other. Shiva's imploring had transformed Ram, and now he was fighting belligerently. Their bodies bled profusely from the fresh wounds that were being delivered. Shiva showed no mercy or restraint towards his student, who managed to dodge his deadly moves while trying to retaliate with full force. And then it happened! The moment Ram had been waiting for, which took Shiva completely by surprise.

Ram carved a painful gnash on Shiva's right upper body. Shiva writhed in pain, momentarily distracted as he held his right hand over the wound. Taking advantage of the situation, Ram catapulted himself through the air a second time. And this time, he did not miss.

The cleaver hit the forehead of Shiva hard, exposing his skull, and was stuck a few centimetres away from the metaphorical third eye. Gnashing his teeth, Ram tried to remove his weapon while hitting Shiva continuously with his left fist. Shiva raised his hand signalling the end of the fight. But Ram didn't notice it in his frenzy.

"Stop," Shiva cried. Ram's raised fist froze mid-air on hearing his master's command.

With one hand raised indicating Ram to stop, Shiva jostled with the other to remove the axe from his forehead. The axe had gouged a deep cut on his forehead while copious amounts of blood oozed from the wound. Removing the axe, he handed it over to Ram who gazed in shock at the bloodied mess.

"This, Parshu, will bring glory to you. I am grateful to have taught a student like you, Parshuram," Shiva addressed his student in a proud voice.

Hot tears were flowing from Ram's eyes. He tore the end of his *angavastram* and started wiping the blood from Shiva's forehead.

"And from now on, the world shall remember me as Khandaparshu, one wounded by an axe," Shiva said embracing Parshuram. A sense of guilt had descended over Parshuram for injuring his master. Though wounded himself, his tears drenched Shiva's skin. Shiva smiled on seeing the plight of his student. He knew the amount of respect Parshuram held for him. He tried to free himself from Ram's tight embrace but Parshu was not ready to let go.

"It is ok, my son. Sharpen your anger and train your mind to control it. Direct it towards your enemies in its full might," Shiva kept whispering encouraging words into Parshu's ears, but his embrace only became tighter. He was having difficulty breathing. After the long and gruesome fight, he needed some rest and attention to his wounds. The blood hadn't ceased flowing from Shiva's forehead. He knew what he had to do to free himself from Parshu. He said in a low voice, "The wound is hurting me, Parshu. A bucketful of cold water would help ease my pain."

Parshu left in a jiffy. Shiva tried to relax his muscles which had become sore under Parshu's tight embrace. In no time, the student returned carrying two buckets of ice-cold water. Shiva smiled. He placed his student's axe in one of the buckets and wiped it clean. Handing it over to Parshuram, he said, "While this will protect you from any attack at close quarters, Pinaka would help you take your enemies by surprise," he said pointing towards the bow.

Parshuram was amazed at his master's generosity. Pinaka had been with Shiva since time immemorial. Its twang had been philosophized by some as the cause for the origin of the universe; the eternal sound; the mother through whose womb all other sounds originate from; the heartbeat of the universe; the *beej mantra*; one resembling the reverberation of *aum* which flowed through every moment, through every atom, reminding it of its indefatigable bond with *Brahman*. Shiva had won countless battles with it. Keeping the axe aside, Parshu fell flat on his mentor's feet. Shiva patted Parshu's head and directed him to pick up the bow that now belonged to him.

"It is my duty to give you *Guru Dakshina*," Parshu forced a few words from his choked throat, "Ask, master, what you want from this lowly student of yours?"

"There is nothing I wish to possess which I do not already have," Shiva said smiling. "You will be known for your anger, Parshu. Use it wisely." Shiva gave one last advice to his student and directed him towards the bow.

It was too heavy for Parshu. He used all his strength to lift the Pinaka but to his surprise, he didn't succeed. Just before the fight, he had seen Shiva wield it effortlessly outside the cave.

"You need to use your heart instead of your head." Parshu heard his master's instructions. He invoked a silent prayer in respect of his master and tried to lift the Pinaka again. The bow melded cleanly into his grip, almost as if it were designed for his smaller than usual hands. He picked it up and stretched the taut string. Pointing it towards the sun, he released it.

"You have hereby inherited the heaviest bow in the whole universe," Shiva declared, "and you are only the second person who has released this divine sound by plucking its bowstring."

Parshu ran his fingers along the wood. It felt quite different from the bows he had seen to date. It seemed to respond to his touch, almost like it shared an inanimate bond with Parshu.

"It cannot be broken, at least, from what I know," Shiva laughed on seeing Parshu observing it.

In Malana, Jamdagni's meditation was broken on hearing the sound reverberating through the air. The energy it carried seemed to resonate with all living and non-living beings. Jamdagni felt it travelling through his own body. It had entered through his ears and was now enveloping his whole mind. All other sounds around him were voided. It seemed to be the only sound filling the entire universe at that moment. He smiled. After many years, his son's training was complete. Now, he could look forward to his return.

SAMVAD

"Can you look into the future?" Ram asked.

Shiva smiled, "Why do you ask that?"

"The master holds all the strings, my father used to say," Ram said.

Shiva laughed, shaking his head in dissent. "Jamdagni has a penchant to dramatize things. All humans have free will. How could anyone predict their behaviour?"

"But my mother believed you," Ram reminded Shiva of his promise to Renuka.

"It has been more than eight months since I started training you. Do you think I could remain true to the promise I made to your mother?" Shiva turned the tables.

Ram felt the nervous energy building inside him. In a weak voice, he replied, "I won't disappoint you."

Shiva laughed, "That is what I expect from you. And then, Renuka would say I predicted the future correctly."

Ram pondered for a moment, "But I have heard so many anecdotes."

Shiva looked towards the sky. "I take my chances. Strong men have strong ambitions. I am good at identifying such strong men. They try to overcome gargantuan obstacles in their path through their sheer will. But in that process, they might turn pompous. The evil in their hearts might run amok, destroying anything that lies in their path. A man must try to remain free from conjuring a larger than life image of himself."

"But there are so many stories about your omnipotence," Parshu's line of questioning continued.

Shiva looked at Parshu, "Because I deal with strong men and women.

They are the ones who can make or break histories. It is their circumstance, actions, and life-events that determine the path of human civilisation. I understand their psyche and motivations."

"So, you know who will rise in their lives," said Ram.

"And who will fall," Shiva said completing Ram's thoughts.

JAMDAGNI

Kartavirya Arjun entered deep into the forest with his entourage. Though it was winter, the royals had decided to head north where it was freezing cold. They had travelled for many days into the forests, in search of a shy, but a dangerous animal – the snow leopard. As the name suggested, the leopard preferred to reside in the solitude of the mountains and was spotted seldom. Its shiny, white fur blended well with the snow during winters, providing an appreciable camouflage. The weather was too cold to bear. But as per king's orders, the entourage trudged on, the deceptive beast still befuddling their eyes.

"I almost want it to attack us. It has been days since we have been walking through this drudge," commented one of the soldiers to his fellowmen.

The place they had reached was covered with layers of snow that completely submerged their boots. The whiteness which enveloped them was bewitching. It dazzled against the sun and hurt their eyes. Many walked with eyes shaded, loosely holding onto their spears. The soldiers were tired from their long journey and wanted to return home. They hadn't eaten proper meals for many days. Their generals forced them to slash through the thick snow, though what they craved at that moment was a warm bed. Few even looked to their commanders with imploring eyes, but all they got in return were looks of resignation. The commanders were bound by the orders of their king. Like the soldiers, they were praying to the forest Gods to help them capture the leopard so they could return home.

Everywhere they looked, the snowy background painted a grim picture. It was the perfect turf for the leopard; the snow-clad mountains were his territory. The king and his royals had been to several forests and had killed a variety of animals; each one more challenging to spot than others, but the snow leopard still eluded them. It was not the first time that Arjun had tasked himself with hunting the white-furred animal. The dried leather of the leopard still eluded his collection at the palace. While the eyes and ears of the king and other royals riding their chariot remained attentive to any kind of movement, the soldiers were left wondering why a king with access to all luxuries of a palace would abandon everything to travel to this discomforting, albeit, life-threatening environment. The few who had accompanied their king on his earlier expeditions, had returned exasperated and empty-handed. They trudged wearily with the group, half-knowing they would return without success this time as well. Never mind killing the leopard, they hadn't even spotted it the last time they had ventured to this part of the country.

But they were soon proved wrong. The beast stole behind them stealthily and attacked. The soldiers were alerted only after hearing the screams of their fellowmen. Before they could react, the body was dragged into a nearby dense overgrowth. They waited with bated breaths for a second attack, their fingers tightly gripping their swords' hilt, but the beast seemed to have sensed their alertness. For a few minutes, the entourage stood still, feeling the cold wind lash against their bristling skin. Just when they thought the leopard was nowhere to be seen, the beast launched another surprise attack from the front. For a moment, its high-pitched growl pierced the silence of the jungle as the leopard leapt towards them, slashing one of the soldiers with its claws while landing heavily on two others.

"Is there just one or an entire pride?" the Haiyaya general sitting atop the elephant's back cried, his sword drawn and ready to attack. He ordered the soldiers at the end to draw their shields and provide cover for the group. Turning his attention towards the king, he commanded a quarter of them to render cover to his chariot. However, before he could complete the tornado of instructions, the group's attention was diverted to the commotion behind them. The general grimaced when he saw someone playing against his strategy at the critical moment. The king had decided to cut through the group and move ahead.

Kartavirya Arjun's chariot had reached the front which remained unguarded from all sides. He refused to take cover. The entourage watched in rapt attention as the king ordered them to remain silent. He kept shifting his weight from one side to the other, looking for any movement which might indicate the leopard's position in the dense undergrowth. Suddenly, his ears caught the rustling of leaves to his left. He watched intently, gauging the speed and direction of the movement before firing an arrow. No sound emanated from the bush suggesting the arrow had missed the target. He placed another arrow against his bowstring and stood awaiting the indications of movement. Seconds turned to minutes, but it seemed the leopard understood he was being watched. The entourage slowly began to lose interest in the whole setting. Arjun kept his gaze to his left, when he suddenly noticed movement at the corner of his eye, and saw a body hurling towards him at a great speed. He turned to face it, but it was too late.

It was larger than a normal leopard, which probably weighed more than half a quintal. It leapt into the air, flying over the horses tied to Arjun's chariot, its gaze concentrated on the king. In less than a second, it was about to land right on top of him. Arjun felt time slowing around him. He could see his reflection in the cold, grey eyes of the beast. The leopard raised his right paw and aimed for the head of the king, who stood frozen in his position. Almost by reflex, Arjun raised his left hand to shield his face, which was covered with the golden, polished arm guard. The sheen of gold reflected against the unblemished skin of the leopard. Arjun blinked just as a spear appeared in his line of vision. He could hear the feeble whistling it made while cutting through the air. He saw the beast turn its head mid-air towards the direction of its nemesis. But it was too late to change course. The spear buried itself just below the leopard's ribs, slicing through its stomach and reappearing on the other side. The leopard missed its target due to the impact and fell writhing in pain at Arjun's side inside the chariot.

The leaves rustled again and out emerged a wise-looking sage from the same direction. Arjun bowed his head in respect.

"Who are you, *Maharishi*?" Arjun asked reverentially.

"Jamdagni," the heavily bearded man said, "Can you ask your soldiers to bring the leopard to my abode? The weather has turned too cold this year. It will provide my children with some much-needed warmth," the sage's face broke into a smile, "Would like to skin it before the flesh gets rotten."

"I will bring it on my own," Arjun answered folding his palms respectfully. The palace would have to wait for the snow leopard's skin to adorn its walls. This one was going to his saviour.

The Brahmin nodded and started moving towards his *ashram* while Arjun's entourage followed him.

***

The *ashram* was not too far away from where the leopard was killed. The sage had cleared a large tract of the forest to provide shelter to his family. Arjun could see a small field covered in snow, waiting for the summers to commence when it could provide for the family. A small shelter was built in one corner. It acted as a storehouse which provided the essential needs during rough weather. Directly opposite to it was a cowshed where Arjun could see the cattle belonging to the sage observing the intruders, whilst calmly chewing the cud.

Jamdagni asked the troops to wait outside the *ashram*. "My modest dwelling cannot accommodate such a large army," he said smiling,

"But, *Maharaj*, my family will be grateful if you can bless them with your auspicious presence," he said to Arjun.

Arjun disembarked and asked his general to bring the dead leopard which was lying at the back of his chariot. Carrying the carcass in his hands, he followed Jamdagni into the *ashram*. He had already removed the spear from its body and handed it to Jamdagni before they had marched to his *ashram*. Once inside, he laid it down on the snow-covered ground near the cowshed and accompanied Jamdagni to meet the family.

Jamdagni knocked on the closed door. A sleepy Renuka emerged, assuming it was her husband who had returned from his morning walk. She was surprised to find another visitor accompanying him so early in the morning. She quickly adjusted her dress as Jamdagni introduced Arjun, the mightiest king of *Bharatvarsh*. She called out to her children. With eyes still groggy from sleep as the cold morning set in, they joined their parents in welcoming the honoured guest to their household.

Arjun entered Jamdagni's house and sat on the floor as Renuka and her children served him breakfast. Considering the meal to be too simple for a king, Renuka busied herself in the kitchen to prepare a few more dishes. Jamdagni understood her mood and waited patiently in a corner for her instructions. He tried to help but Renuka's angry glances were enough to discourage him from being of use. Without prior information, her husband had bought a guest to their home, and that too, a king of repute.

"Where is Vasu?" Renuka suddenly remembered. She wanted her eldest son to meet the king too. Finally, Jamdagni had a task at hand. He went out and looked for him. Vasu was busy tending to the cows in the shed. He called out to his son, asking him to quickly return to the house.

Vasu came running from the cowshed. He looked around and was puzzled to see a large army stationed outside. He entered his home and looked at his father quizzically. With an encouraging nod, Jamdagni directed him to touch Arjun's feet who was busy finishing the soup Renuka had served. Vasu bowed and reached towards the king's feet when his father caught his hand mid-way.

"What were you up to?" he asked sternly, looking at the blackened palms of Vasu.

"A cow had injured her leg yesterday. I was applying some ointment on her wound," Vasu said sincerely.

"And you were about to apply some of it on my feet," Arjun looked sternly towards the young man. Vasu stood apologetically looking at his father, his hands still held firmly by Jamdagni.

Arjun burst out laughing looking at the slightly embarrassed Jamdagni, "No need for such formalities. It is I who breached your privacy and should apologise." He looked towards Renuka and thanked her for the meal, "We should be leaving soon. Your husband saved my life today and I couldn't refuse his invitation to accompany him to his home. I will ask my general to prepare the troops for our return."

"Not before they have had their fill. They have travelled a long distance and I could see from their faces that they need some nutrition. The weather here is rough. Let me prepare something for your journey back. Your capital is quite far from here," Renuka said.

"I don't think that is necessary." Though moved by their hospitality, Arjun was unsure if such a modest household would have the means to serve so many of his soldiers. Politely refusing the invitation was the only way to not embarrass the family, he thought.

"Don't worry about that, *Maharaj*. Come, I will show you around," Jamdagni said delightedly. The excitement of hosting the Mahismati king was largely evident on his face.

Arjun was amused and didn't protest further. He couldn't see how his troop of five hundred could be served. But he decided to go with it. After all, Jamdagni was his saviour. There was no point in holding anything against him if his family faltered in serving his famished army.

"It would be my pleasure. But not before I have finished the task I am here for," he said and asked Renuka for a cleaver.

With a broad, sharpened knife in hand, Arjun went with Jamdagni and started skinning the leopard. He removed his headgear, armour, and the heavy ornaments that adorned him, and set about his task. His years of living as an ascetic had taught him a few lessons on surviving with frugal supplies, and using every resource provided by nature. He cut open the smooth and supple skin of the leopard and cleanly removed all its organs. He washed the blood and hung the skin to dry. Close to an hour had passed before he finished the task. Arjun was sweating profusely by then, his whole body covered in leopard's blood mixed with his perspiration. The stench hung heavily on his clothes. He asked Jamdagni to guide him to a place where he could clean himself.

"I hope the household is not overwhelmed by the presence of so many soldiers. I saw your children serving them sweetmeats. You don't need to worry about our *sevabhagat*. They are a self-sufficient unit who can take care of themselves," Arjun repeated his apprehension, being mindful about not offending the sage.

"Nothing to worry about, *Rajan*," Jamdagni smiled, "It is an honour for me and my family to have the privilege of serving the strongest man on earth. And don't fret about your company. A household blessed by Kamdhenu cannot be troubled by the number of guests."

"What is Kamdhenu?" Arjun was intrigued. He wanted to know the sage's secret.

"Not what; who?" Jamdagni laughed. He didn't feel the need to hide anything from such a great king. "She was a gift from Indra, the king of the *devas*. When I moved to Malana, owing to the rough weather, the Gods gifted us with their benevolence. You can take your bath," said Jamdagni pointing towards a well at one end of his *ashram*, "and then I shall show you the cowshed and Kamdhenu."

Lunch was prepared by the time Arjun was done with cleaning himself. His soldiers had gorged themselves on sweetmeats and other delicacies, and now, they had very little appetite left for the hot lunch which was being served. He could see many of them lolling around, enjoying the sunny afternoon. A well-fed stomach and the chance to bask in the sun after an arduous journey was eternal bliss. A special seat was arranged for Arjun, his general, and the other people of eminence inside Jamdagni's house. The officers sat awaiting the king's arrival before they could partake in the lunch, the aroma of which made many of them salivate. Over the last few days, they had been bereft of such a splendid spread.

The food prepared was simple but tasteful; a plateful of chapatis, *daal*, curry and salad followed by serving of rice and *kheer*. Arjun, along with the others, ate to his heart's content. As promised, the sage's family had been able to provide for the whole entourage. Everyone in his group was surprised by the feat. But sages around the country were known for miracles. He thanked the couple for the sumptuous food and informed them of their leave.

"We would like to traverse some distance before the sun sets," he said.

"But you haven't seen the Kamdhenu yet?" Jamdagni remarked.

Arjun laughed, "Sorry, the sumptuous food made me forget everything."

Both men walked towards the cowshed where Kamdhenu resided and welcomed them with her mooing. Whatever little excitement Arjun held of witnessing Kamdhenu was drained as soon as he entered the shed. Standing before him was a herd of morose looking cows tied close to each other and among them stood Kamdhenu, no different than the others. Tied to one end of the wooden stake, she was blithely chewing the cud and using her tail to swat the flies. Arjun looked towards his host with mock interest. He was still unsure if that was what Jamdagni wanted to show him.

"It seems she doesn't find us interesting," said Arjun.

"Yes, but you will find her interesting," Jamdagni smiled, "Haven't you heard about *samudra manthan*?"

It was an old story Arjun had heard as a child. He had forgotten it but Jamdagni's mention of *samudra manthan* awakened his memories. The personification of mother earth, the fulfiller of everything a man can desire, the mother of all cattle was standing before him. He reverentially bowed his head towards the Godmother, Kamdhenu.

"So, it is true?" he asked. Jamdagni stood smiling, looking at the surprised face of the king. "The *samudra manthan*, it did happen?" Arjun's curiosity was piqued.

"Every night you see the proof of it," Jamdagni said pointing towards the sky. Arjun thought for a moment and understood that the sage was referring to the moon.

"Is it true what we know about Kamdhenu?" Arjun's trail of questions continued.

"Yes, she provides more than what you ask for. How else do you think a puny Brahmin like me could provide for a battalion of royal soldiers?" Jamdagni touched his palms in a reverential *pranam* before Kamdhenu.

Jamdagni was a *saptarshi*. To assume he was playing with one's senses would be a folly. The hostile surroundings of Malana didn't have much vegetation to boast of. Like an oasis in the desert stood Jamdagni's *ashram*, entirely due to Kamdhenu.

"Should I ask for a few offerings from the mother?" Arjun wanted to test Kamdhenu's prowess.

"You don't believe me," Jamdagni said in a comforting tone. Arjun's face flushed. He quickly apologised for his trepidation and asked for the sage's leave. They walked towards the *ashram*'s gates where the Mahismati's soldiers were waiting for their king.

For the next couple of minutes, Arjun remained lost in his thoughts, 'A fulfilling life without worrying about the future – this is the greatest gift Kamdhenu bestows upon its owner. Jamdagni's family has everything one could ask for. A boon worth fighting for!'

With their appetite satiated, the soldiers looked cheerful and ready for some adventure. Meghraj looked towards Arjun, indicating it was time to leave. Arjun nodded as he turned to thank Jamdagni's family for its hospitality. No one could mistake the anxiety on his face. It seemed the king wanted to ask something but was tongue-tied at the thought. Jamdagni was amused looking at Arjun who was palpitating. The king was spasming, seemingly out of some agony clawing at his heart.

Finally, Arjun said, "I have a favour to ask."

"The mightiest king needs a poor sage's favour," Jamdagni smiled, "It will be an honour, *Rajan*."

"Do not be offended, but I would like to request you to endow me with Kamdhenu's blessings. I wish to take her with me. It would prove to be a boon for my poor subjects. Millions of impoverished citizens could be provided for. Every year, thousands of my subjects succumb to starvation. I would be able to provide my citizens with a minimum standard of living. Kamdhenu can solve that puzzle for us.

Also, it would add to your glory, sage Jamdagni. I would make sure that everyone knows it was you who helped bring prosperity to Mahismati," Arjun said. His face had turned quite red. The contentedness of Jamdagni seemed to be worth vying for.

It was an awkward request; more so that it was coming from the most powerful king of the *Bharatvarsh*. Jamdagni tried to remain gentle in his reply, "It is not mine to give, *Maharaj*. Kamdhenu is a divine cow. A mortal sage like myself cannot decide where she should live. Her home depends on her desires. It was gifted to me by Indra. I am grateful to him for choosing me to bestow his blessings. It would be an insult to him if I do not ask for his permission before parting with her. Nevertheless, while I am afraid I must deny your request, you and your troops are welcome to Malana anytime you choose. Rest assured, Kamdhenu won't shy away from serving you."

"But you don't understand," Arjun continued trying to make Jamdagni see the obvious, "here, Kamdhenu is catering to the needs of a small family but in my kingdom, it would be able to serve the entire citizenry. It will act as a safety net for millions of people. Her potential is not fully utilised here."

"Is this the reason you are asking for Kamdhenu?" said Jamdagni observing the king. Though perturbed, he tried to keep his voice calm, "She is the divine mother and not some efficient machine, *Rajan*."

Arjun could sense signs of protest in the sage's voice. He thought for a moment and said, "I believe it is one of the most logical requests I have ever made to anyone. And believe me, I haven't had to ask for many things in my life. I can give you a great price for Kamdhenu if that is what you are looking for, sage Jamdagni. You and your family can accompany my entourage to Mahismati and I will appoint you to the royal court. Tell me, sage, what it is that you want, and I will make sure you get much more than that."

In his life, Jamdagni had met many kings with bloated egos. He knew a straight refusal might anger Arjun.

"In exchange, I want half your kingdom," Jamdagni said pensively.

Arjun laughed, "That is too hefty a price for a mere cow."

"Do you believe Kamdhenu's value to be less than that?" Jamdagni asked. A worried Renuka looked towards her husband. She was unsure where the conversation was headed.

Arjun was not amused and repeated himself, "Ask for a legitimate price and you shall have it."

"I have another way to settle the debate. Part with half of your treasury, distribute it among your people and then come back to discuss Kamdhenu with me. Doing this would be a great help to your subjects," Jamdagni said.

Arjun felt that the sage was trying to get his goat. He was used to people following his commands without questioning them. He couldn't remember a time when he'd wanted something and hadn't received it in earnest.

"I think you are missing my point, *Rajan*," Jamdagni continued, "There are many other legitimate ways to serve your people, but you are not interested in any of them. You are too attached to your throne and your accumulated wealth, and don't want to part with any of it. Yet you ask a poor sage to part with the only possession of value he has."

Arjun looked at Jamdagni sternly. He was losing his patience. "I understand what you are trying to say, Brahmin. But as a Haiyaya king, I order you to hand over the Kamdhenu. It belongs to Mahismati now."

But Jamdagni too had decided not to give up easily, "I saved your life. My family served your entourage, and this is how you decide to return our hospitality. A bit of modesty would suit you well, king.

Kamdhenu doesn't belong to anyone but the Gods. She is as much of Mahismati as the mother Earth."

Arjun grimaced. The snow leopard had been killed, and like his soldiers, he too wanted to return home.

"Don't force me to commit a crime, sage," Arjun said. Jamdagni stared at him with cold eyes. There was no point in picking a fight with an armed battalion of Mahismati. On receiving no reply from the sage, Arjun asked Meghraj to bring Kamdhenu from the cowshed.

"You won't benefit from this wretchedness, king. You are trying to bring happiness to your subjects by making others suffer," It was Renuka who, amidst the collective shrieks of her family, addressed the king as they saw the general following his king's orders.

Arjun laughed, "You should ask your husband to be more accommodating in the future."

The four sons looked at their father for instructions. The well-trained youths were ready to fight but Jamdagni wouldn't allow them to. There were at least five hundred armed men standing in front of his *ashram*.

The sage's sons were young and proud. The insult to their father was too much for them. Vasu, the eldest, took hold of the nearest soldier. Before his opponent could react, Vasu reached for his sword and removed it from its sheath, Arjun cast his arms wide open and invited Vasu to try it on him instead, laughing menacingly. Vasu stood his ground with the soldier wincing under his hold. Seeing Arjun draw his sword, Vasu aimed for his chest, but Arjun caught his blade mid-air with his free hand. He raised his fist and punched the young man hard between his ribs. Vasu fell on the ground, gasping for air. His sword landed many feet away owing to the impact. The soldier who was unarmed, was soon joined by others who started kicking him wildly and spat on his face. Jamdagni dropped down and tried to cover his son, but the Mahismati soldiers didn't stop their assault.

"Don't you dare raise a hand on our guests," Renuka's cry was heard over the mayhem. Her other sons looked ready to join the fight. Hearing their mother, however, they stopped in their tracks.

"Forgive us, king," she pleaded to Arjun, "Take whatever you want but spare my family."

Arjun smiled and looked towards Renuka but didn't order his soldiers to stop. He then turned his gaze to her other sons, each one of whom seemed ready to gauge the king's eyes out.

"Ask for the king's forgiveness," Renuka knew what the king was looking for. The brothers reluctantly bowed their heads.

Arjun saw his general return, with Kamdhenu calmly following him.

"Stop," he cried climbing onto his chariot.

The soldiers dispersed. Vasu had fainted by then. Jamdagni held his head on his lap and patted him softly. Kamdhenu turned her head to look towards Renuka who stood stoically. She watched as the general handed her leash to a soldier standing in front, while taking his position with the entourage.

"Kamdhenu will return to me, *Rajan*," Jamdagni said, his back facing Arjun.

Arjun chariot was turning away from his *ashram*, "You can live in your wishful world, sage. Time will tell the virtuous deed you accomplished today by deciding to part with Kamdhenu."

"It was not in my power to decide," Jamdagni laughed, "Time will surely tell, *Rajan*."

Jamdagni turned towards the soldier who was holding Kamdhenu, "It is quite a long journey. Ask your men to take some hay too. It is lying in the cowshed." But the soldier didn't have time to follow the sage's advice. He left with the group while the entire family bid a teary-eyed farewell to Kamdhenu.

***

The journey towards Malana was long but Parshu had never felt better. He was able to cover many miles every day owing to the downhill path. Images of his family flashed in his mind. He couldn't wait to meet them. He kept smiling, remembering the childhood memories of his brothers practicing in the training ground while he used to cower because of his insecurities.

'I believe I would be a tough rival for each of them now,' he made a mental note to compete with each of his brothers using their favoured weapons. 'Now they won't be able to make fun of their little brother.' A wide smile crossed his lips as he was lost in his thoughts.

In a few days, he reached his home and found the wooden gates guarding the *ashram* left open. That was strange! He remembered how his mother had been very particular about keeping them closed at all times. She had chided her sons a thousand times for it.

"You want a lion to wander in and eat you up. Or worse, he attacks the cowshed," Renuka would say.

He entered his house and saw his family huddled together with long faces. Vasu was lying on the floor being tended to by his mother.

"What happened?" Parshu asked to no one particular. The smile had vanished from his face.

Renuka lifted her eyes and was moved to tears to see her baby boy back after so many years. She took him in her tight embrace.

"Where have you been, Ram?" she asked, her voice hoarse.

Ram watched his elder brother from the corner of his eye. It looked like some beast had mauled him. Renuka was applying some ointment on the black marks near his ribs where the blood had clotted. His eyes were still fearful, indicating he hadn't recovered from the shock yet. His other brothers looked equally moved due to some incident that had happened in his absence.

His eyes searched for his father who was sat quietly in a corner. A wry smile resided on Jamdagni's face when their eyes met. His face, too, was clouded by sadness.

"Who did this?" Parshu hissed looking at his father.

Jamdagni remained calm. He approached Ram who was still clinging to his mother. Freeing himself from his mother's embrace, Ram touched his father's feet. Pulling him up, Jamdagni said, "You must be tired from the long journey. Go, take some rest, son. We have a lot to catch up on. It has been so many years."

Ram then touched Vasu's feet though he seemed to be asleep. Then he went towards his other brothers who huddled around the youngest one. They had missed him sorely.

"What has Lord Shiva done to you? We had sent him the best of our lot. Did you not eat anything these last four years?" Brutwakanwa teased Ram.

For some time, the brothers made small talk and laughed together. They talked about the lost years and about how each of them had fared. They gave a detailed account of everything that had happened; how they'd built the boundary around the *ashram's* perimeter, where the latest fields they'd bought under cultivation were, and how the number of cattle in the shed had almost doubled.

"How is Kamdhenu?" Ram suddenly remembered.

A pall of gloom descended on the faces of Ram's brothers. Parshu looked to his father who had also been enjoying his sons' conversation, but now, looked to the ground shamefaced. Ram understood he had touched a raw nerve. Picking up his axe, he moved to the shed.

Kamdhenu's place of rest was in shambles. It seemed someone had tried to forcibly move her out. The other cows were visibly perturbed and stood in rapt attention without touching even a blade of grass laid before them. Ram went back to his family. He saw his father crying softly.

"He took her away from us, son. Vasu tried to stop him, but he couldn't," Jamdagni said pointing towards his son, "He was too strong for us. Thankfully, he left us alive."

Even in the coldness of Malana, Ram felt his body heat up. He saw his father cry for the first time in his life and it was not a pleasant sight. He looked at his brothers and asked, "Who did this?"

"Kartavirya Arjun," replied Brutwakanwa.

Without a word, Ram went to his father and touched his feet. Then, he left for Mahismati. Jamdagni understood what was going through his youngest son's mind.

"Stay for a few more days, son," Ram heard Jamdagni's cry from behind. But it didn't deter him. The image of his father crying overpowered his senses.

'I was late by a day or I could have prevented this from happening,' he thought. A feeling of guilt invaded Ram's heart. He had to avenge his father's insult at the hands of Arjun.

Ram had wanted to rest his tired feet when he had reached home, but he ignored his weariness and continued walking towards the Haiyaya capital. During the nights, the image of Jamdagni's face awash with tears came back to haunt him every time he tried to close his eyes.

In the next few days, Ram reached Mahismati, which was built on the banks of the river Narmada. But it would not be an easy feat to reach the king. Mahismati was heavily guarded. A short-statured, powerfully built man armed with an oversized axe and an intricately designed bow was bound to be viewed with suspicion. But Ram's *janeu*, the mark of a Brahmin, allowed him to move around a bit freely.

Mahismati was a rich and resplendent city and its markets were vibrant. Most of its places were newly constructed and inhabited, and the city attracted migrants from various parts of the kingdom owing to the immense opportunities it provided. Ram soaked himself in the exquisiteness of the city for a while. He saw the lively food markets with people jostling for space and ordering food from their favourite shops. He also saw large houses of the royalty, guarded by burly men who could strike fear into the hearts of trespassers. He maneuvered through the narrow lanes of the colonies where abject poverty and contagious diseases ran amok; where the hollowed, dreamless eyes of children, adults, and the old stared at him.

In a couple of days, Ram got to know from a man selling silverware in the city market that a royal *sabha* was held once every week, which was presided by the king himself. It was the only time when the common man was allowed a glimpse of their king. The *sabha* sounded like the perfect opening for Ram. He decided to wait for it and took a room at the local *Dharamshala*. For the next few days, Mahismati witnessed a well-built, armed Brahmin walking its streets, with no apparent purpose.

The day scheduled for the *sabha* finally arrived. Parshu had been unable to sleep the whole night as he waited for morning to arrive. As dawn arrived, Ram took a quick bath, remembering his father and his teacher before leaving for the *sabha*. He followed the locals to the palace. A large hall which accommodated at least a few thousands welcomed him. He jostled through the crowd to find a place nearest to the king. A large, white, marble throne placed in the middle adorned the room. In an hour, the room was filled to the brim with people who stood with their bodies brushing against each other. All the eyes were directed towards the throne which was still empty. Parshu looked around and saw a few guards holding prisoners in line, along with other civilians. It seemed to be a line of people who had come to the king to seek justice. Parshu thought about joining them. But he had successfully placed himself near the king's throne. He decided to stay there and let the *sabha* know about his presence when the time came. Half an hour or so passed when the crowd suddenly started to cheer. Kartavirya Arjun entered the hall followed by his royal entourage. He greeted the onlookers before taking his seat. With a clap of his hands, he directed the *sabha* to commence.

The proceedings for the day began in earnest. The king had received the schedule for the day from his advisors in the morning. More than a thousand cases were filed to the Mahismati royal court every week. The cases were prioritised based on merit and only a few were given consideration by the king's advisors, which became part of the weekly proceedings. Despite that, the king's court was affected by pendency. The cases were complex, and Arjun took his job quite seriously. He never hurried in ruling judgment unless he was certain he had examined all the facts.

People who had been waiting in line started approaching Arjun in an orderly manner. Over the next three hours, the king remained busy with dispensing justice. Parshu listened intently to the proceedings along with the others there. He was impressed by the inquisitiveness Arjun applied to each of the cases. It was a rare day when the line of people who sought justice almost reached its end.

"Would I get representation before the king?" Parshu's voice boomed over the *sabha*.

All the eyes turned towards the Brahmin. Bearing an axe, he looked like a man who needed to be taken seriously. Arjun smiled looking at Ram. It was rare for someone to have the courage to interrupt his proceedings.

"Mahismati bears a large heart to accommodate everyone. Come forward, sage. We are grateful to have you in our company," Arjun said, before adding, "Though I would hear this as a one-off case, my humble request to the citizens of our state is to refrain from such disruptions." The sternness in his voice was evident.

Parshu reached the centre of the hall. The guards came forward and asked him to disarm himself. It was not safe to have a man bearing weapons so close to the royal courtiers. Parshu glared at them angrily. He was in no mood to part with it.

"It's alright, soldiers. The Brahmin is our guest. Treat him with respect," Arjun commanded looking at Parshu.

Parshu turned his attention towards the king, "I have come here for justice, *Rajan*. One of the citizens of Mahismati has stolen my belongings, injured my loved ones, and vandalised my household."

Arjun listened to the Brahmin intently. 'What valuables could a poor Brahmin have that could be stolen,' he thought to himself.

"My family tried to stop him, but he overpowered them along with his accomplices," Parshu continued.

"What was it that was stolen, *Rishi*?" Arjun asked.

"We will come to that later. Let me ask you this: what is the quantum of punishment for such a crime?" Parshu questioned.

Arjun was not used to hearing such questions, nor was he liable to answer. But the Brahmin had a determined look on his face. His serious baritone demanded answers.

"Well, was someone killed or maimed in the incident?" Arjun asked.

"No," Parshu answered.

"But people were injured, and articles were stolen. Your family had to face material loss," Arjun said.

"Yes," said Parshu.

"I need to look into the details of the incident but based on what you say, it seems your family was the victim of thievery. Mahismati has decreed to cut off the hands of thieves or dacoits," Arjun said.

"Then, so be it," Parshu's grip on his axe tightened.

"Unless the person is ready to return your valuables and take care of the damages," Arjun added thoughtfully.

"And what if he refuses?" Parshu asked.

"Then the law takes its course," Arjun said.

Parshu thought for a moment and then asked, "*Maharaj*, has an accused ever refused to acknowledge the rule of law in this court? What if you or your court is unable to apprehend him for his crime?"

Arjun guffawed, "No one is above the law in Mahismati, Brahmin. Rest assured, you will not be denied justice. If the one you accuse is truly guilty, I empower you to invite him for a trial by combat," Arjun mocked, sizing the short stature of Parshu, "I, Arjun, will fight for you if you develop cold feet."

Parshu was amused on hearing Arjun refer to himself in the third person. He continued, looking sternly at the king, "I am here for Kamdhenu, Kartavirya Arjun."

Arjun watched the Brahmin in silence for a while. He was impressed by his confidence. Not once did he blink while accusing the mightiest king of the *Bharatvarsh* with theft. A bemused smile creased his lips.

"I envy your courage, sage. It seems you have the blood of Jamdagni flowing through your veins. I had tried to reason with your family. Are you a son of Jamdagni?" he asked looking at Ram's youthfulness.

"Yes, Parshuram," said Parshu, "and I am here to take back what is rightfully mine."

Arjun laughed hysterically, "Kamdhenu belongs to no one. It is God's gift to mankind. By claiming to be its owner, you are dishonouring humanity."

"And by stealing it, have you done a great favour to it?" Ram retorted sarcastically.

The whole *sabha* was stunned. No one dared to talk to the king that way. They waited for Arjun to speak while his sharp gaze glared at Parshu.

"How do you feel, Arjun, about judging people for their crimes while overlooking one of your own? What punishment do you suggest for your crime?" Parshu continued.

"Brahmin, you have created enough ruckus for the day. Your father was quite hospitable to me and my soldiers, even though his sons were foolish enough to confront them. Because of that, I ask that you leave respectfully," Arjun was losing his patience.

"Does Mahismati refuse to provide justice to me?" Ram remained insistent.

The whole *sabha* waited with bated breaths. While Arjun was amused by the Brahmin's courage, he was not sure about what he wanted. He tried a direct approach.

"My army confiscated Kamdhenu for the benefit of Mahismati. On one hand, I can see how beneficial it would be for my subjects, and on the other stands your selfish interests. I refuse to part with it since I believe Kamdhenu would be of greater value here," Arjun stated.

The soldiers slowly approached from both sides to remove Ram forcefully from the court, if needed. Ram sensed their movement but stood his ground. As a soldier on his right tried to grab his arm, he yielded a stern look, "Dare to touch me and it will be your last day on this earth."

Somehow, the soldier knew the Brahmin was not joking. He looked towards his master, the king, for instructions.

It was then that Arjun lost his cool. He had entertained the Brahmin for too long. Up until then, he had empathised with him because, deep down, he knew how he must have felt on seeing his distraught parents. But he didn't want someone to get the better of him in front of his own people. He decided to put the Brahmin in his place. "You should be grateful, son of Jamdagni, that the mightiest king of Bharat allowed such insinuations. This would turn out to be one of the high points of your life. You should return to your homeland and tell your friends in the years to come about how, one day, you stood before Kartavirya Arjun and he bestowed you an audience. I command you to not invite my wrath and leave this court quickly, or Mahismati will have to forget how it treats its guests."

But Ram didn't budge. "I want Kamdhenu back," he repeated.

Arjun laughed, "I think the naked beggar has gone crazy. He keeps repeating himself," he addressed the public.

"I want a trial by combat," the sonorous booming voice of Parshu could be heard above the collective, amused giggles in the audience.

"You want to be killed?" Arjun was shaking with anger now. The crowd turned silent and waited wordlessly for the events to unfold.

"No, I want to kill the thief as per the law of Mahismati," Parshu said calmly.

Arjun, exasperated from the exchange, climbed down his throne and removed his sword from the hilt. "If that is what you want."

Dragging the sword across the stairs so that the metal rattled against the ground, Arjun bought himself to face Parshu. Parshu was almost half his stature and a quarter of his girth, but he didn't flinch. Under Shiva's tutelage, he had faced *Rakshashas* much larger in size. He waited for Arjun to deliver the first blow.

"What do you desire to convey to your family if you lose this fight?" Arjun asked.

"Tell them I died for their honour. But what if you lose?" Parshu asked.

Arjun smiled. "Then you will become the master of everything I own," he said, giving his sword a forceful swing.

Arjun was a trained warrior. His initial attack took Parshu by surprise. He didn't aim for his head or his heart; rather, he tried to wound his lower body. Parshu wasn't prepared for it. Showing great agility, he swiftly moved back, but the sharp blade still wrecked a nasty gash on his lower thigh. Parshu tried to regain his balance but Arjun pushed him onto the ground. Dropping his sword, he started pounding him with his fists. Arjun seemed too strong for him. A few from the crowd expressed their pity for the Brahmin. They dreaded seeing a sad and murky end to this faceoff. Arjun's punches stopped when Parshu's whimpers became evident. He got to his feet and waited for the Brahmin to move. Seeing Parshu crawling towards his axe, he spat on his face and made his way back to his throne.

"Pick up your weapon, *Rajan*," Arjun heard a voice calling him from behind, "I don't want to fight an unarmed man."

Arjun's face turned red with anger. He picked up his sword and ran menacingly towards Parshu who was still lying on the floor, his fingers clutching his axe. Having been beaten black and blue, he seemed to have lost the strength to stand. Arjun aimed for his neck. He wanted to end Parshu's suffering quickly. But suddenly, Parshu's hands moved. The sword clanged against his axe. Parshu was able to block Arjun's attack using his axe. Resplendent with anger, Arjun's sword whistled through the air but was blocked a second time. Parshu remained lying on the floor but didn't allow Arjun to fatally wound him. The gory dance went on for what seemed like an eternity. Arjun kept trying to get past Parshu's axe which deftly blocked him. Beads of sweat lined Arjun's forehead as he was beginning to get tired of this ordeal. The court watched in awe as Parshu, bereft of any strength even to stand, defended himself against a buffed-up Arjun. As his hands grew tired from the swinging, Arjun raised his feet to crush Parshu. That was the opening Parshu was waiting for. A sharp cry of pain made the audience gasp as a strong jab from Parshu made his axe strike Arjun's sole.

Arjun reeled from the impact, but Parshu struck again, this time aiming his axe at his shin. Blood began to flow profusely from the open wound. Arjun fell heavily on the ground next to Parshu. Taking advantage of this, Ram started hacking away at Arjun's body without pause. The whole court was stunned into silence on seeing the short Brahmin puncturing their king's body with multiple wounds. Arjun was in no position to defend himself. Parshu, though devoid of strength, worked furiously with his axe, and finally, dealt the fatal strike to Arjun's neck.

Ram remained motionless for a while, trying to recover some of his strength to pick himself up. Mahismati had just lost its king. Karta-virya Arjun, the man with a thousand arms and the strength of a hun-dred elephants, lay dead on the ground. His subjects remained glued to their seats, unsure of how to react. All eyes moved towards the Mahismati general as he started moving. The general looked at the severed head of Arjun for a while and then extended his hands to pick Ram up.

"All hail Parshuram, the new king of Mahismati," he announced in a loud voice. The audience was shaken out of their reverie. They started chanting Ram's name as he stood precariously supported by the gen-eral. Once the chanting ceased, Parshuram asked for some water and took a seat on an empty chair nearby. He looked towards the throne of Mahismati. His father had asked Arjun to part with half of it. The throne that had seen the most powerful rulers, who had not been afraid to challenge even the Gods, belonged to Parshuram now. There were multiple wounds on Ram's torso which still bled non-stop. It would take time for them to heal. He took a few minutes to catch his breath before turning his attention towards the axe which was stuck to the now severed head.

Parshu went and tried to remove it. But it seemed to be rammed in too deep. Parshu used his entire strength holding the joint where the blade was molded into the arm. Suddenly, the joint moved to reveal a narrow opening. Trying not to surprise the others who were watching his actions, Parshu picked up a small parchment which had fallen out of that opening. Giving a sudden jolt to the blade, he clicked the opening shut. Holding the axe against his shoulders, he walked towards the throne of Mahismati. The king's chair was made of pure gold. Clutching the parchment in his hand, Parshu took his seat on the throne. Placing his axe on the wide armrest, he addressed the court which was waiting to hear from its new king.

"I am no king," Parshu said. His voice was too feeble to be heard by everyone. The fight with Arjun had been quite taxing for him. Parshu raised his voice which sounded hoarse even to his ears, "I am not here to become a king. I am here for Kamdhenu."

"As per the rules of the duel, you are our new king. Not only Kamdhenu, but everything within the boundary of Mahismati belongs to you," the Mahismati general said. He directed one of his soldiers to bring Kamdhenu.

"The throne belongs to its people. I didn't come here to become a king. I am a Brahmin by birth and do not wish to usurp the role of the Kshatriyas. My request was simple," Parshu looked towards Arjun's severed head; its eyes stared into his.

"Son, if you are going to renounce the throne, you need to appoint someone as its ruler," it was the head priest of Mahismati.

Ram thought for a while and then said, "Let the court decide its ruler. I open the post of the king to all the commoners who are gathered here today. Let us elect our leader. Anyone who thinks he is worthy of the throne can stand for it."

Such a process was unheard of. The head priest was astonished, "This has never happened before. The subjects are barely aware of what goes into ruling a kingdom. How can they vote for a king?"

"What hasn't happened to date, will happen now. Let Mahismati become an example for the whole world. Who wants to nominate himself for the post of the king?" Ram asked the gathering.

"But…," the priest tried to interject again.

"This will be the last time you interrupt your king," Ram glared at the priest who bowed his head in deference.

The people gathered around took time to digest what was being asked of them. They were overwhelmed by the happenings of the day. The court proceeding which was a routine affair was about to witness three different kings of Mahismati in succession. As the crowd looked on, they saw a few hands go up. Ram asked the people who had raised their hands to come forward.

"I also want to contest," a voice distracted him. He looked at the man in shackles. Earlier that morning, Arjun had asked the man to be imprisoned for a petty crime. Though all the evidence had pointed to his guilt, the man hadn't confessed it. Ram thought for a moment and then directed the soldiers to free the man so he could stand in line with the other contestants.

"Your majesty, he is a criminal. He can't be considered for the post," it was Meghraj who exclaimed in disbelief.

"Everyone should be given the chance to atone for his sins. In my eyes, even your last king had committed a grave crime. In comparison, this one has been charged with stealing a few crumbs of bread," Ram said.

"In that case, the prisons of Mahismati are filled with people who have committed similar crimes or are guilty of lesser crimes," the head priest said.

Ram stood up from the throne and announced, "Let it be known that from this day forth, Mahismati shall embark on a journey which would benefit each one of its citizens. The king waives all taxes for this year which are yet to be collected by the administration. Release all the prisoners despite whatever crimes they may have committed. From this day forth, all administrative decisions will be taken by the majority through a secret vote. Let us open the royal expenses and revenue for public scrutiny."

It was easier said than done, and Ram knew it too. As the voting for the new king commenced, Ram looked towards the contestants and said, "Whoever among you becomes the new king of Mahismati, you can be assured of my return if any of these tenets are violated."

The candidates nodded their heads in haste. The large axe Ram held was still soaked in blood. Over the next few hours, Ram presided over choosing the king. Once the new king assumed the throne of Mahismati, Ram left the hall with Kamdhenu following him. His work at Mahismati was completed. It was time to return to his parents.

Parshu looked at the parchment clenched in his fist. The soft paper was soaked in Ram's blood, but the name written in large letters was still quite clear. In black ink was written a single word, the name of the previous ruler of Mahismati, 'Arjun'. 'So, he knew,' Parshu smiled. Throwing away the parchment after shredding it, Parshu made his way towards Malana, wondering what secret Pinaka might be holding.

"The weapons would reveal their true purpose when the time comes. You don't have to force anything out of them," his master's words echoed in his ears.

'Let the opportune time arrive,' thought Parshu like the faithful student that he was.

PARSHU

Ram still remembered the following months clearly. He had just killed one of the mightiest warriors, someone who had been revered throughout the country. As expected, his fame grew by leaps and bounds after that incident. People from all walks of life started visiting Malana to seek his blessings. A recluse by nature, Parshuram tried to avoid such meetings, but with so many followers, he found it difficult to be left alone. Men, women, and children from all over the country wanted to know more about the slayer of the man with a thousand arms.

Ram, the youngest of the family, had suddenly turned into somebody. The family too was overwhelmed by the endless stream of people arriving to meet him.

He remembered the pride on his father's face when he returned with Kamdhenu. Jamdagni and the others were stunned to hear that he had killed Arjun. The powerful king living comfortably in his four-walled fortress, protected by thousands of his soldiers, was killed by a common Brahmin. It was a fete unheard of.

"Shiva was right in his assessment," said Renuka, holding Ram in a tight embrace.

"And you were not," Jamdagni said laughing.

"I came to Malana to seek solitude and found it many years ago. Your fame has rendered my quest fruitless," Jamdagni began complaining to his son as people from all walks of life started thronging to his *ashram*, seeking Ram's blessings. Though, in his heart, he was quite proud of his son's accomplishment. Not everyone would go the distance to fight for his father's pride.

And for a few years hence, Ram lived happily with his family in their modest household. All the five brothers practiced at the training ground together in the morning. Later, they cleaned the *ashram* and prepared the platform used by Jamdagni and Renuka to perform their daily *yagna*. They had decided to take on the burden of overseeing the household, freeing their parents who were now growing old. Collecting dried wood and meat, cultivating the farmlands, tending to the cows, and other such tasks were divided among the brothers. A small hut was constructed a little further from the *ashram*. Visitors who arrived to meet Ram were directed towards the hut. Ram spent most of his day meditating in the hut. Most of his devotees reached Malana after a long sojourn. Ram made sure every one of them returned with their appetite satiated.

"Kamdhenu hasn't had a chance to rest even for a day since her return," Vasu would remark in jest, "she might lose her patience continuously serving the pot-bellied devotees of a reed-thin Brahmin."

***

Summer was approaching. The weather in Malana had changed for the better. The snow thawed while the brothers spent most of their time on the farms. It was on one such morning that Ram, along with his brothers, had gone into the forest. It took them longer than usual. Even after a couple of hours, they hadn't tasted success. Back home, Jamdagni was seated in front of the fire altar having completed his morning ablutions. It was a few days before the auspicious period of *Navratri*, a festival celebrated in veneration of Goddess Durga. In the upcoming nine-day period, the family was planning to hold a fast to appease the Goddess. They were looking forward to gorging themselves before the fast. The sons were out in the forest, looking for the tasteful meat of a white-bellied musk deer.

A sudden commotion in the forest shook Jamdagni out of his reverie.

Initially, he thought it was his sons who had returned from their jaunt. But he soon realised it was the sound of horse's hooves striking against the forest ground. It seemed a small troop was approaching the *ashram* on horseback. Renuka was still inside the house. Jamdagni called out to his sons assuming one of them might be around. Getting no response, he decided to investigate the matter himself. He went to the *ashram's* entrance and bolted it from inside. The sound of approaching hooves was getting louder. In a couple of minutes, he saw a flag bearing Haiyaya colours moving towards his *ashram*. The riders were approaching at breakneck speed. Something seemed amiss to Jamdagni. He was not sure what Mahismati wanted from him. Worried about Renuka, he tried to rush back inside the house. But the horsemen were quick. They busted through the *ashram's* entrance and surrounded the unarmed Jamdagni.

"Do you remember my son?" Jamdagni glared at them with anger. Instead of answering his question, one of the horsemen brought out his sword and slashed hard from behind. A searing pain in his back affirmed Jamdagni of Mahismati's intentions. He suppressed his cry of pain as he didn't want to startle Renuka. He took hold of the armour of one of the soldiers mounted on the horse and brought him to the ground. He wrestled to wrench the sword out of the soldier's hands. Though the soldier's strength was drained from the fall, he did not give up easily. After slicing his neck, Jamdagni turned his attention to the others. One by one, the Haiyaya soldiers started plopping on the ground after facing his attacks. Their cries filled the land and alerted Renuka of the attack. She came running out of the house. The scene in front of her was overwhelming. She supported herself against a pillar and started crying, her voice hoarse with anguish. In a cracking tone, she kept imploring the Mahismati soldiers to stop their attacks. The dead bodies piled around Jamdagni. But it seemed he was fighting an endless line of soldiers. One of the soldiers tossed a lasso towards Jamdagni. The rope entwined his well-built body. Jamdagni tried to move but the noose around him tightened. The lasso rendered him immobile. Taking advantage, the other soldiers bound him with ropes. They took him to the fire altar and tied him to one of the pillars. Jamdagni was bleeding profusely and felt he might faint.

"You thought Mahismati will forgive you," a voice boomed from behind.

A shorter, less-wider version of Kartavirya Arjun emerged from behind. Surrounded by burly men on both sides, the man walked towards Jamdagni, unsheathing a knife.

"We are the sons of Kartavirya Arjun," one of the heavy-set men said. Jamdagni knew there was no point in arguing with them. He gave a resigned look to the three brothers and waited for the pain to recede. With a practiced hand, the man in the middle started carving his body with the knife. The other two brothers watched the proceedings calmly. Renuka's cries reverberated through the forest, but to no avail. Jamdagni's life soon escaped his body, but the man did not cease his onslaught. He kept slashing the lifeless body for another few minutes while Renuka fainted.

It was an hour later when Ram returned. The shock of seeing their father tied, bloodied, and dead was too much for Vasu who'd fainted at the entrance. While his other brothers ran towards their father's corpse, Ram went to his mother who was still lying on the ground. Renuka was back to her senses, supporting herself against a pillar. Ram placed her head on his lap. He brought some water in a flask and made her drink it. Dried tears streaked Renuka's cheeks as she stared into oblivion. She kept murmuring something to herself continuously. Ram had difficulty hearing her. He looked towards her lips trying to decipher what she was saying. It was only one word that Renuka kept repeating, 'Jama.'

"Who did this, mother?" Ram asked calmly. Though shaken to the core, he didn't want to add to his mother's grief. Renuka looked at him with expressionless eyes. Then she searched for her other sons. She saw that they had already untied and washed their father's body and were preparing it for his cremation.

"Who did this, mother?" Ram asked again. Renuka's eyes were transfixed on Jamdagni's face.

"Arjun's sons. There were three of them. They didn't ask Jama too many questions. They tied him using a rope and started butchering him," her eyes turned towards Ram, "Your father fought bravely. But they were too many. They surrounded him like a swarm of bees and attacked with all kinds of weapons. As soon as they introduced themselves, Jama knew they would kill him."

Taking his mother by the arm, Ram walked to a nearby clearing where Jamdagni's pyre was being prepared. Jamdagni's face glowed under the bright sun as his body lay covered by a white sheet, all signs of violence washed away. A strong wind was blowing through the mountains. The mother-son duo sat silently, looking into the void, as the other brothers collected dry wood from the nearby forest. The surroundings which had witnessed the gruesome violence a few hours ago stood calmly, watching the family coping with their misery.

Vasu had revived by then. He was busy lighting a torch at a distance. In a few hours, the sons carried their father's body and placed it on a platform of dry wood. They poured *ghee* over it as Vasu circled the pyre with a burning torch in his hand. Ram saw his eldest brother snivelling. His other brothers were equally distraught. A sense of guilt pricked his conscience. He had never imagined killing Arjun would lead to his father's murder.

The flames leapt towards the sky as Vasu threw the lighted torch into the pyre; the black smoke enveloping the clean mountain air. The brothers stood in silence, shaken by the whole incidence. Kamdhenu's constant baying broke through the monotony. Brutwakanwa went to the cowshed as the mooing grew shrill. The other brothers joined Ram and their mother. Renuka's tears had subsided by then. The hot air rising from the pyre had dried them; thick lines of salt marked her cheeks. She sat, bereft of any strength, the misery sapping it away as she rested her head against Ram's shoulders.

"It was because of me," Ram said voicing his inner turmoil.

None of the brothers responded for a while. Each one was fighting his own guilt.

"Father had asked me not to go to the jungles today. He needed my help in cleaning the *ashram*," said Brihudyanu, "but I promised to do it once I returned from the hunt."

"None of you are at fault," Renuka said in a weak voice with her eyes closed, "If not Jama, then it would have been some other sage."

"Arjun visited our *ashram* and forcefully took Kamdhenu, our only treasured possession," she continued, "a fear-mongering, armed group, led by the king's sons, killed Jama in cold blood. The Kshatriyas feel entitled to such murderous whims. They think anything they set their sights on belongs to them. They commit violence without remorse."

Ram had heard instances of the Kshatriya chieftains acting as dictators against their citizens. Even during calamities, they wouldn't reduce the taxes and their soldiers would mercilessly whip the farmers to extract their dues. Few of them even terrorized the village women, their lustful eyes always in search of prey. They delayed undertaking development works and ignored the well-being of their subjects, while building huge palaces for themselves without an ounce of conscience. Many Kshatriya kings and princes thought they owned the lives of the common masses and any protests, however legitimate, which reared its head against them needed to be crushed mercilessly.

"What if I hadn't killed Arjun?" Ram asked.

"Then the insult of being unable to save your family's honour and helplessly watching the dacoits destroy your household would still be alive," it was Vasu who replied, "You didn't go to Mahismati to kill Arjun. It was his arrogance which killed him. You only wanted Kamdhenu back. And had Arjun parted with it peacefully, you wouldn't have caused any harm. Like him, his sons were brash enough to think that they could enter the *ashram* of any puny Brahmin and claim ownership over his property, family, and life."

"It is not about your father anymore, Ram," Renuka looked into his eyes, "It is about freeing the minds and souls of people from fear. A few tyrants cannot remain in control of the lives of millions of people. We need better people to rule us."

Parshuram looked towards his father's pyre. The wood was crackling under the fire. "I would provide them with better people, better Kshatriyas," he said, "and it will start with the sons of Kartavirya Arjun."

***

It was almost evening. All his brothers, along with Renuka, had left for their home as it was getting cold. Ram sat alone, looking at the burnt remains of his father.

"Don't scatter my ashes in the waters of river Ganga," Jamdagni used to say. As was customary for a Brahmin, the family members dispersed the cremated remains of their relatives in the holy river. "Let the wind blow me away. If not in this life, then maybe after my death, I would be able to reach Kailash's summit."

Towards the horizon, Ram saw a lone figure making his way towards the fire. The lean frame holding the trident looked as anguished as he was. He too had lost one of his favourite students. A deep furrow marked his forehead; the third eye ready to flicker. Parshuram stood up as he approached.

Shiva embraced Parshuram, trying to assuage his sorrows. "Don't let your anger dissipate or defeat you," he said in a hoarse voice sitting next to him.

"You have warned me a thousand times," Parshuram smiled, "my anger will die with me, but first, it shall burn the high pedestals of the Kshatriyas."

Shiva looked teary-eyed at his student. Any son would be angry at the world in such circumstances. But he felt Parshuram's words emanated from somewhere deep.

"It is the Kshatriyas who have brought ruin to my family and the world. I will make this earth bereft of them and cleanse their evils. That is my life's mission now," Shiva heard Parshuram mumbling under his breath.

Shiva squeezed Parshuram's hands softly. He didn't want to impose his whims on someone who had just lost his father. An unshakable resolve was etched onto his grief-stricken face.

"Give it some time. It will subside," he said. For the next few days, Shiva stayed with Parshuram's family, sharing in their sorrows. He waited patiently for them to absorb the shock of the tragedy.

***

On his last day at Malana, he bid farewell to Parshuram who was at the training ground sharpening his axe.

"Take care, son," Shiva said, "there is no point bearing so much hatred in your heart for the world."

"Not for the world," said Parshuram, "but for the kings and the princes. Kshatriya kings, and no other; this was my oath to my dead father."

Even after so many days, Parshuram remained adamant.

"One who conquers his emotions wins all battles," he said.

Parshuram laughed, "Rest assured, I will only wield your weapons to protect *Dharm*."

Shiva replied, the hurt visible in his words, "Let the axe stay with you on this journey. I must, however, request you to hand over the bow."

Parshu looked into his master's eyes. It seemed he was trying to hide something from his student.

"You don't believe that I would be able to fulfil it," he asked.

The master laughed, "You can fulfil it a hundred times over, Parshuram. But you have chosen this axe for your life's journey. Hand me the Pinaka. It was not meant for you."

"You gave that bow to me for a purpose. Do you believe I am not capable of it now?" Parshuram was heartbroken seeing Shiva asking him to part with it.

'Why must emotions run so high with all my students?' Shiva thought. He weighed his words carefully, "I believe in you, more than anyone else. You are the only one in the entire universe who waged a commendable fight with Khandaparshu. I would be questioning my teachings if I doubted your abilities. But since you have chosen this treacherous journey for yourself, the Pinaka might act as an obstacle in it. As your teacher, I command you to hand over the bow to someone you think might be worthy of it. Let the world remember you for your axe."

'After all, the weapons belong to him,' thought Parshuram. With a respectful glint in his eye, he said, "It is my utmost duty to follow my master's command. From now on, Pinaka shall be off-limits for me."

Shiva smiled and asked for Parshu's permission to leave. He went towards Renuka and said, "You are a proud mother of a Brahmin among Brahmins. Parshuram will be remembered as one of the finest Brahmins who stood against evil," were his parting words.

***

Once the rituals related to Jamdagni's death were over, it was time for Parshuram to return to Mahismati. His brothers implored him to allow them to accompany him, but he resisted. Despite being the youngest amongst his brothers, Parshuram was by far the most adamant.

"You might have to face the entire army of Mahismati," said Vasu.

"That was a risk I took the last time as well," Parshuram laughed as he started on foot, "Our mother needs most of her sons alive, and after all, it was my fault that the Haiyaya Kshatriyas attacked our father." The sorrow from Jamdagni's murder was too strong for the fort walls to bear. The soldiers of Mahismati still remembered how Parshuram had killed their emperor who was considered invincible by many. The guards at the fort's parapet saw the sage approaching the city gates; his axe shining in the broad daylight. While a few of them laid down their arms, some others ran in haste to inform their general.

"Parshuram is back. The erstwhile king of Mahismati is waiting at the gates," one of the soldiers shrieked as soon as he saw Meghraj. The general of the Mahismati army was inspecting the armoury. He was not surprised listening to his subordinate.

"The last time he came here, he sought revenge because the king stole his father's cow. What would one have expected?" Meghraj said smiling while accompanying the soldier to his station.

"I am here for the sons of Kartavirya Arjun," Parshuram hissed once the general of Mahismati went down on his knees in front of him, "I do not have any other qualms. Just hand them over to me."

Meghraj took out a scroll stamped with the seal of the Mahismati kingdom and handed it over to Parshuram. Parshuram read through the contents of the scroll.

'The kingdom of Mahismati hereby denounces any association with Kartavirya Arjun and his relations. Any action sage Parshuram takes against them would be deemed fit,' the scroll mentioned.

"They have been given official quarters next to the palace," said Meghraj referring to Arjun's sons, "Saumukh was torn between his duties when he heard about the incident. He knew you wouldn't remain silent after that. But Mahismati has been ruled by Arjun and his ancestors for centuries. Any adverse action by him against the dynasty would be viewed as a conspiracy."

Saumukh had been elected king of Mahismati the day Parshuram had killed Arjun. Meghraj asked a few soldiers to escort Parshuram to the place where the brothers lived. Parshuram waited patiently outside as the soldiers went to inform Arjun's sons of his arrival.

Within an hour, the three sons of Kartavirya Arjun appeared to face the dreaded Brahmin. They were armed to the hilt. Parshuram's eyes glinted dangerously on seeing the prey make their way to him. Drawing their swords while riding their horses, they surrounded Parshuram from all sides.

"No armour?" sneered the eldest, looking at the Brahmin standing rigid, with just the sacred thread adorning his upper body, "We would break you like a twig."

"It would have impeded my movements," the sage smiled.

Parshuram stretched his left leg out in front, pointing towards the eldest one, while shifting his weight to the right knee. He bent his upper body and brought the arm holding the axe in line with the other brother. Curving the fingers of his left hand in a bear claw, he directed it towards the youngest among them. "Marjaravadivu," hissed Parshuram. It was the stance of a cat.

"Kalarippayattu," the youngest of the lot whispered, "the Brahmin seems to be trained in lethal martial arts." Parshuram stood in rapt attention waiting for the brothers to attack.

As the brother began striking, the sage jumped, ducked, whirled, kicked, punched and hacked; all too quickly. The sons of Kartavirya Arjun weren't prepared for someone who was so light on his feet. Their heavy armours made it difficult to follow Parshuram's moves. To an observer, he seemed to be floating in mid-air most of the time. They tried to use their weapons to defend themselves but in vain. Even with his short frame, Parshuram was able to jump on and over the horses to nullify the advantage of the riders.

The three were trained warriors and fought valiantly. But like their father, they too met their demise.

Once his business in Mahismati was taken care of, Parshuram travelled further south. There were others who had to be dispensed with. For years he busied himself with challenging the powerful kings across the country. By that point, he had commandeered a small army of his own. They were branded as 'bandits' by rulers who were the target of their wrath. Parshuram established many Kalaris – the training places for Kalarippayattu where these so-called bandits were taught to fight with the deadliest weapons. Through his efforts, Kalarippayattu, the mother of all martial arts, became institutionalised. Unbeknownst to him, as Shiva has prophesied, the legacy of Parshuram remains alive even after thousands of years.

His battles soon became part of the folklore. People couldn't remember a period in history when so much blood had flowed on the battlefields. Kings who were famed for their savagery were beheaded by his axe. He battled against the best of the lot. He fought against powerful kings and chiefs, who hadn't batted an eyelid while wiping out entire villages, on charges of treason. He stood against those dictators whose armies exploited its citizens while ruling with an iron fist. He humbled the proud emperors who built formidable forts and maintained large armies at the expense of their poor subjects.

Such were Parshuram's stories that it struck fear into the hearts of children and adults alike. However, the line between the good and evil Kshatriyas became dimmed with time. Even a few kings who were viewed as good leaders in the eyes of the subjects were killed. Few were brought to justice for trivial crimes.

"Revenge has consumed him," some would say.

"A heartless vigilante is as dangerous as a stupid king," said the others.

***

Bhadra sat on his throne oozing blood. Sleep was knocking on his door, but he tried to remain in his senses. He knew he wouldn't return if he fell asleep. The short-statured sage sat at one corner of his court. He, too, was fatigued after such a long duel. A bowl full of water, now turned red, was in front of him. He sat cleaning his axe calmly.

"What for?" asked Bhadra. It was a large hall. His voice couldn't reach the Brahmin's ears.

"What about my family?" Bhadra tried to muster some strength.

The Brahmin looked at his victim. He knew he was about to lose himself to the oblivion.

"Their personal grief stands nowhere in comparison to what you have done to others," said the Brahmin.

"What have I done?" asked Bhadra.

"Remained adamant with your tax demands months after month, made the children and the old toil mercilessly in the fields, threatened villagers with dire consequences if they quit - the list is quite long, Bhadra. Do you have any idea how many children died working in the fields under the scorching heat? Your soldiers would beat them ruthlessly if they wanted to rest," Parshuram said, his axe gleaming.

Bhadra remained motionless for a few moments. He spoke again with much effort. Froth oozed from his lips, "You beheaded Lakshya too a few weeks ago."

"Yes, for similar reasons," Parshuram replied calmly.

Bhadra laughed, "It is because of you. We are paying for your sins."

Parshuram looked at him with a puzzled expression. He always tried to listen to his victims on their deathbed. Most of them had a lot to repent for.

"Heard about Ravan? His felony surpasses your imagination. Evil is running amok through the veins of mother earth because of your doing, Parshu," Bhadra said in a malevolent tone, "I made them work long hours; he makes them work until it kills them. I make the children toil; his soldiers hunt newborn non- *Rakshasha* children. I threaten, they slaughter," Bhadra said.

Parshuram laughed, "Don't blame your sins on others, Bhadra."

"I needed to secure my territory. Ravan's army is a threat to our kingdoms. All the revenue my kingdom produces goes straight into strengthening the military. But it is never enough. The bordering villages have already been abandoned due to the *Rakshashas'* threat. Which do you think is worse? To work towards securing the state or dying at the hands of the *Rakshasha*?" Bhadra looked sharply towards Parshuram. The fear was visible in his eyes. "Violence is the only constant which resides under Ravan's rule. His *Rakshasha* troops do not wait for opportunities like droughts or floods to exploit the villagers. Their motive is to subjugate the other races in their territory. His army is ruthless. He usurped the throne of Lanka from his brother. With the blessings of Lord Shiva, he even fought against the Gods."

Parshuram smiled on hearing the name of his teacher, "Interesting! He must have fought many brave kings on the battlefield."

"Quite a few, but none were able to defeat him," said Bhadra. He gazed intently at Parshuram, "Except one. If only Kartavirya Arjun had been alive."

Bhadra had caught Parshuram by surprise, "He was the only king who halted his advances. The earth revelled in peace during the years Ravan lolled in the prisons of Mahismati. But the maniac is free now and his rage knows no bounds."

"When was he set free?" Parshuram could not hide the guilt on his face.

Bhadra laughed spitting blood. He was delighted to see the sage reeling under his barbs.

"The wheel of time makes you revisit the long-forgotten past, Parshuram," he remarked, "It is time to right those wrongs. It was your orders that allowed Ravan to roam freely in this world and to cause havoc."

"I will make him pay for his sins. Tomorrow, I will commence my march towards Lanka," Parshuram said while trying to remain calm.

"You took up this task to cleanse the world and ended up making it worse," Bhadra stuttered.

"What is done cannot be undone. The emperors of *Bharatvarsh* treat the *Rakshashas* as outcastes but their women are not off-limits," said Parshuram thoughtfully.

"You won't be able to defeat him," said Bhadra.

"My axe would see to that. Many held a similar opinion about you and the other Kshatriya kings I have killed. It was not his mother, but the seeds of his father which had turned him into a monster," said Parshuram, assuming Ravan was the progeny of a Kshatriya king.

"A Brahmin by birth, sage Vishrava is his father," Bhadra wheezed. His end was near. Parshuram's grip on the axe momentarily weakened.

For a few moments, Parshuram remained lost in his thoughts. He looked up and saw the light dim from Bhadra's eyes. In the last few minutes, everything that had been viewed as black and white by the Brahmin had suddenly turned grey. 'It is a treacherous path towards righteousness. One can only seek to achieve balance in the world,' his master's voice echoed.

"I made a promise to my father," the sage whispered.

He stood up and slowly walked out of the court. His legs seemed to be drained of any strength. The weight of his deeds over the last few years seemed too heavy on his shoulders.

Parshuram spent the next few months acquiring information about Ravan. It was not only in Bhadra's kingdom, but the threat seemed to loom large over the whole of *Bharatvarsh*. The *Rakshasha* pride knew no bounds. 'Bow or bury' was the motto of Ravan's army. All the non-*Rakshasha* races in his kingdom were treated as second class citizens with no rights to call their own. Anyone who rebelled against the rule was killed over the slightest doubts. This progeny of a Brahmin seemed to have turned against his people; his biggest target being the Brahmins.

Parshuram returned to his family in Malana; a faraway land where it would be difficult for news of Ravan to reach his ears. He disbanded his army, a few of whom remained his followers. He established an *ashram* that trained Brahmin students in the art of warfare and wielded his axe only when he was convinced of someone's pleas for protection.

"I was tending to the blemishes while the mutilation was oozing pus," he used to remark whenever somebody enquired about his past life. And now, after so many years, it was time to atone for his sins. Tadka had died at the hands of Ram. Pinaka was waiting for its true bearer. The rebalance had begun.

VISHVAMITR

- 196 -

Vishvamitr was quite happy with his new students. Troubled by the *Rakshashas*, he had gone to king Dashrath to seek help in getting rid of them. Dashrath welcomed him to Ayodhya and asked his eldest son, Ram, to accompany the sage to the jungle. Lakshman, the younger son, joined at the hip to Ram, pleaded to be able to join his elder brother in the quest. Vishvamitr led the two brave sons of Ayodhya to his *ashram* located on the boundary of Tadka *van*.

The company of the brothers proved to be quite enterprising. Under the tutelage of Vishvamitr, they had learned to wield celestial weapons and use them effectively against the *Rakshashas*. They helped the sages continue their rituals, fearlessly guarding their *ashrams* against any surprise attacks. The area which had been feared and loathed by many, was slowly turning into a place of solace for the peaceful sages.

"Parshuram has come to meet you," said one *shishya* to Vishvamitr who was busy cleaning his room. It was one of his daily tasks. He joined his students in cleaning the whole *ashram* every morning.

Vishvamitr went outside to greet Parshuram. "Come, my son," he said hugging Parshuram warmly. The two held each other in a tight embrace for a few moments. Vishvamitr was delighted to meet his grandnephew after many years.

Parshuram's father, Jamdagni, was the son of Satyavati, Vishvamitr's elder sister. Belonging to the same clan, both sages were stalwarts of their era. Vishvamitr, renowned for his Brahmanical traits, was a Kshatriya by birth, born to king Gaadhi of Kanyakubj, while Parshu, the son of a Brahmin, was known for his Kshatriya traits. The world recognized them for their incredible feats. Vishvamitr was a *Brahmarshi*, the highest pedestal a sage could hope to attain in his lifetime. He had contributed greatly to the Rig Veda, the holy book containing the first sermons of the Sanatan *Dharm*. He had also authored the *Gayatri Mantra*, the most revered mantra which is still recited before every *yagna*.

A popular folklore about him alluded to his status in the minds of people. Erstwhile King Trishanku had requested Vishvamitr to allow him to enter heaven while he was alive. Vishvamitr seeing the burning desire in Trishanku's eyes acceded to his request and performed the *yagna* to help him attain it. No one had ever managed to enter *Swarg* in their bodily form. Indra, the king of Gods, refused Trishanku's entry. This enraged Vishvamitr who turned his fury against the Gods. Such was his reputation that people believed after his altercation with Indra, Vishvamitr tasked himself with creating an alternate universe. Furthermore, he also decided to create another Brahma and *Swarg* with Gods of his creation. It was only after Brahma's persuasion that Vishvamitr was pacified and stopped in his quest.

"Parshu won't visit a puny Brahmin without a purpose," said Vishvamitr, the master of a modest *ashram*, and teacher to the, then, famous princes of Ayodhya, Ram and Lakshman, smiling.

Parshuram touched Vishvamitr's feet. After trading information about the happenings in their lives over the last few years, Parshu finally revealed his purpose of visit, "I am here for Ravan."

"I see the guilt still haunts you," Vishvamitr said observing Parshuram closely.

"After so many years, I see a glimmer of hope. I heard about your students who had killed Tadka. Though I am sure, it would not have been possible without your help," Parshu's eyes conveyed his long wait.

Vishvamitr was elated on hearing that the glory brought forth by his students had reached the ears of Parshuram, a warrior without equal.

"Not just Tadka, they killed her son Subahu, too. Though Mareech was successful in his escape," said Vishvamitr looking meaningfully towards Parshuram, "the news must have reached the king of the south by now. It was at his command that the trio had moved so close to the territory of the northern kingdoms. They were a threat to the territory of Ayodhya and Kosala. It was at Dashrath's behest that I commanded the ablest warriors of Ayodhya against the powerful *Rakshashas*."

"I am here to hand over to Ram the bow he deserves. The weapon will reveal its true purpose when the time comes," said Parshuram repeating his master's words. He placed the bow at Vishvamitr's feet.

All it took was one glance and Vishvamitr knew it was no ordinary weapon. He stepped back and bowed his head in respect.

"This is Pinaka," he exclaimed.

"Given to me by Shiva himself," said Parshuram reverentially.

"And you have come here to hand it over to Ram?" Vishvamitr asked, his curiosity knew no bounds.

"As suggested by the master himself. Only a warrior of Ram's caliber is worthy of handling this bow," said Parshuram.

Vishvamitr thought for a moment. Parshuram was right. He could not think of any other warrior in the whole of *Aryavarta* worthy of wielding Shiva's bow. He was still unsure of why Parshuram wanted to part with it. 'The *rishi* must have pondered over this well,' he assumed.

"You are making it too easy for him. He needs to earn it, like Ravan earned the Chandrahaas, rather than bestowing it on him like a blessing," Vishvamitr was known to be hard on his students.

'Anything given for free holds very little value in the hands of its receiver,' Shiva's voice echoed in Parshuram's mind.

"The *swayamvar* for the ablest warrior of Videha is about to take place," Parshuram returned his attention to Vishvamitr.

"Sita," Parshuram said.

"The Pinaka should be dictated as the prize to be won for her hand in marriage. I believe a woman of her stature deserves a test like this," said Vishvamitr.

"I think we would be enacting the toughest test on the suitors," Parshuram laughed before turning thoughtful, "Don't you think Ram is capable of facing the scourge of *Rakshashas* alone? If anything, the killing of Tadka should have convinced you."

"Yes, he is," Vishvamitr said determinately. He seemed to be looking into the future, "But he would need all the help he can get when facing Ravan."

"Would Dashrath agree to this union?" Parshuram asked.

Vishvamitr smiled, "I will talk to Ram's father. I know he won't be too difficult to convince."

"What if someone else wins at this *swayamvar*?" Parshuram wanted to be sure of Vishvamitr's plan.

Vishvamitr reached for the bow lying on the ground. "Don't worry. I don't think it will happen," he laughed as the bow shifted slightly due to his efforts.

Parshuram picked up the bow. He had a long journey ahead towards Videha. But there was still a nagging doubt lingering in his mind.

"What are we setting out to achieve from this? As far as I reckon, Ram wouldn't fare badly in any test we put him through," said Parshuram, "But the mandate from his father was to protect the sages and clear the forests adjoining Ayodhya of *Rakshashas*. It doesn't mean he would be keen on journeying to an unknown land like Lanka to face Ravan."

Vishvamitr smiled, "One step at a time, Parshu. Let us first test his prowess and later watch how Ram's destiny plays out."

It was late evening when Parshu asked for the sage's leave. He had spent the entire day in Vishvamitr's company.

"You have travelled too far. Don't you want to meet the people you are placing your trust in?" Vishvamitr asked.

"No," said Parshuram, "I'd rather wait."

Surya Shrestha came back to haunt his memory. The news of his death was too painful for Parshu. He had become too attached to the favourite student. This time around, he wanted to remain aloof.

***

"I don't want to get married yet," Sita complained to her parents.

"Don't worry. Nothing will change for you. We are simply welcoming another member to our family. You can be just as annoying towards him," her mother retorted.

According to her parents, Sita and her sisters were of marriageable age. Their father, Janak, the king of Videha, was looking for suitable alliances for his daughters. He had planned a *swayamvar* where suitors would compete to win her hand. He was still working on the modalities of the event. Sita was no ordinary woman. Many years ago, Janak had found her abandoned in a field and since then, he had never stopped thanking the Gods for the lucky encounter. From that day forward, Janak's fortunes and repute had increased manifolds; a change of fortune which he owed to Sita.

But finding a befitting competition was not something he had had in his sights. He was looking for something which could astonish his daughter's suitors, and only a man far from the ordinary could accomplish it.

"*Maharaj*, Parshuram is waiting outside the court," Janak had just dismissed his court and was sitting alone on his throne, lost in his thoughts. He was not expecting any visitors.

"Bring him in. You should have done it earlier. Why did you keep him waiting?" Parshuram was notorious for his anger and Janak was in no mood to offend him.

The sage entered carrying a large bow. Janak had never seen a similar bow in his entire life. It seemed to be heavily used but its strings were as taut as new. Carved entirely from wood, the bow was an exquisite masterpiece. Etched on its body were intricate designs of Gods performing different acts of miracle; Indra gliding through the skies on Airavat; Surya riding his golden chariot driven by seven horses; Agni burning the *Rakshashas*, and in the middle was Lord Shiva; away from all the chaos; meditating.

"How have you been, Janak?" Parshuram asked the king.

Janak climbed down his throne. With great adulation, he touched the sage's feet.

"It is the greatest honour for Videha that a sage of your stature has chosen to visit it," Janak said.

The men discussed Videha and its subjects for a few minutes. Parshuram enquired about Janak's family. The king told him he was worried about the marriages of his daughters and wished for them to get betrothed soon.

"I heard about it. The least I can do is offer a solution for the eldest, Sita," Parshuram said pointing towards the bow he was carrying.

Janak listened to him intently. "This is Pinaka," Parshuram continued, "The bow of Shiva; witness to the creation of the universe. I hand this bow over to you, Janak. Any suitor who possesses the ability to bear its weight and hold it high in air would be worthy of being Sita's husband. Send your messengers to distant lands and invite all kings and princes for the competition. I am sure suitors will come in hordes to win the daughters of Videha."

Janak was known to be quite spiritual. He enjoyed spending time in the company of sages and holding philosophical discussions with them. Videha was quite famous for its state-sponsored councils which occurred every year. Sages belonging to different cults and sects arrived to hold discussions about the philosophies of life. Videha's hospitality and Janak's respectful demeanor towards these sages were part of the folklore by then. He found it difficult to deny a request from any sage, and standing before him was Parshuram, the slayer of twenty-one Kshatriya clans. He was afraid to refuse though he felt the test that was proposed was slightly inappropriate for the task at hand; picking up a bow which was slung carelessly on the sage's shoulder didn't seem arduous.

Parshuram sensed Janak's discomfort. "Hold it in your hands," he said, pointing towards the bow still balanced on his right shoulder.

Janak complied. He clenched the bow from the top and tried to raise it. But the bow didn't budge. He tried again and was still unable to move it. Parshuram smiled at him. He asked Janak to use both his hands.

"Now do you believe it will be a worthy competition?" Parshuram asked, seeing Janak struggling with the bow.

Janak nodded. He asked Parshu to place the bow at a corner of the court, on a raised dais which would act as the performance stage during the *swayamvar*.

"It belongs to the master. Handle it with care, Janak. It is too precious to be broken," said Parshuram while placing the bow on the platform.

Janak nodded, "I will protect it with my life."

"There is just one promise I need from you," Parshuram said looking into Janak's eyes.

"Whatever you say, *Maharishi*," said Janak, hanging onto every word intently.

"I don't want a *deva* or a *Rakshasha* to marry your daughter. Let the day of *swayamvar* belong to *Aryavarta*. Our race needs a role model; examples of strong men who can perform impossible feats. Let this competition instill some pride in humanity," he said.

"I will follow your wishes, *Maharishi*. But may I ask the reason behind such a condition?" asked Janak.

"Sita is a blessing from the mother earth to you, Janak. She was found on our lands," Parshuram said, referring to Sita's discovery from a mud pot. "As our race dwells on the same realm, I believe she has a bigger role to play in the history of *Aryavarta*."

Janak bid farewell to Parshuram. Looking at the bow, he muttered a few mantras under his breath. He asked the guards to close the gates of the court once he left. It was time to inform all the kingdoms about Sita's *swayamvar*.

***

Janak's court was filled with suitors. Kings and princes from every corner of *Aryavarta* had arrived to win Sita's hand in marriage. The princess's reputation surpassed most of her suitors. Regarded as a ferocious warrior, Sita had led many expeditions into the nearby jungles of Videha to cleanse them of the *Rakshashas*. Villages that lived in constant fear of having their crops destroyed or their women being kidnapped were living happily once the nuisance was eradicated. Few of the villages had erected temples in her honour. She was a master at wielding swords. Once she mounted a horse, the beautiful radiant Sita acquired a different persona, riding fearlessly across difficult terrains and deep jungles. She was adept at guerrilla warfare and was capable of immobilising large troops through her well-thought-out plans. But at that moment, the lady was decked from head to toe in glistening jewels and a bright red saree. She was seated on a large dais at the top floor of the court, quietly surveying the emperors who had gathered. It was difficult to judge from the appearances who would be most suited to become her husband.

But she had been enamoured by a man she had seen that morning.

Sita had been picking flowers for her daily prayers. It was then that she had noticed two princes, pale and spent, seemingly having traversed a long distance to reach Janakpuri, the capital of Videha, where Janak's palace stood. They were resting in a garden close to the Parvati temple. Offering prayers at the temple was Sita's daily ritual. While returning, she saw the two men who were lying bare-chested in the garden. Well-built and tanned, they were unlike the other princes she had seen till then. Most of them looked like they belonged in the palace; their soft hands, small paunch, and shiny skin bearing proof of it. As someone who preferred the outdoors, Sita was used to the frequent displeasures shown by her mother.

"The earth won't swallow you up if you try to look more like a *Rajku-mari*," her mother would keep repeating. Princesses were known for spending most of their time on their appearances. But Sita loved to wander and roam free; her escapades actively supported by her father.

"Don't you see how no other kingdom in the *Bharatvarsh* can boast of a princess like her? She doesn't need to groom herself for any man; rather, any man would be fortunate to have her as his wife," Janak would say.

And so, standing next to Urmila, her younger sister, a garland in hand, Sita waited with bated breath for the bronze-skinned suitor. She knew the test her father had set was not easy and any man who passed it would be worth his weight in gold. Though, in her heart, she sincerely hoped that the man whose eyes had met hers in the garden would be able to do it.

Tall and thick-bearded, Vishvamitr entered Janak's court with two of his students and was given a seat next to the king. Janakpuri was seldom visited by such knowledgeable sages, and that too, a *brahmarshi*. His two students took their seats among the other suitors. Janak consulted with Vishvamitr regarding the auspicious time for the commencement of the event, and once he received the nod of approval, the competition began. Kings from reputed kingdoms tried their hand at lifting the bow but failed miserably. None were able to move it by even an inch. Even the giant of a man, the prince of Kuru was sweating profusely, muttering under his breath. Following him came a prince adept at sorcery and magic.

"I hope he is able to lift it," Urmila teased Sita seeing the prince examining the bow.

Sita was amused by seeing the prince trying to move the bow from a distance. After every failed attempt, he would circle the stage trying to invoke the strength of the invisible Gods, only to fail again. Then there were others who searched for a hidden mechanism to pick the bow up. Some tried to pick it up from one end, while a few used all their strength in pulling the taut string, but the bow refused to budge. At last, Sita saw Ram walk towards the bow, a diminutive smile on his face. A silent prayer escaped her lips to Goddess Parvati, the consort of Shiva, hoping for the man in front of her to succeed. Ram reached for the bow and prayed to Shiva, the destroyer, to bestow him with strength. He looked around the court. The gathering had lost interest in the competition by then. 'Janak doesn't want his daughter to get married,' he had heard someone mention a while ago. He circled the stage once, quietly observing the weapon. Turning towards the *sabha*, he said, "You need to use your heart." He held the bow from the middle and picked it up effortlessly.

The bow fit his hand perfectly. Ram looked intently at its carvings. An expert artisan had built the bow in earnest. He tried to gauge its weight. While the ends were quite heavy, the bow seemed to be quite light at the centre.

'It is hollow from inside,' Ram clutched the bow at its centre. He gave a slight jolt and felt something move inside. Keeping a firm grip on the middle using one hand, he pulled at the end which pointed upwards. The bow cracked into two, the string snapping with a loud twang and revealing an opening at the centre.

"He broke the bow," someone exclaimed. Since even picking up the bow was surprising to them, someone breaking it was astounding. The whole court was filled with a cacophony of sounds.

"I heard it belonged to Shiva. He had invited his wrath upon him," someone said.

"Must be a God himself to do such a thing," said another.

Ram was also astonished by seeing how the bow had responded. He knew he had not broken the weapon. It had been designed to reveal the opening. Turning it upside down, he gave it a gentle shake and a piece of parchment fell onto his hand. He was distracted by a movement across the staircase in the court. He looked up to see Sita descending the stairs coyly. He hid the parchment between his fingers and placed the now 'broken' bow back onto the dais. He beamed on looking at his bride to be and thanked his stars for helping him find her.

***

The *Rakshasha* limped towards the palace of Lanka. He had covered a long distance to reach his motherland. Even though many days had passed, his wounds still looked fresh. But deeper were the wounds that had been etched in his heart. A few months prior, he had contemplated revolting against his brother for his mother's kingdom. But as fate would have it, he had lost everything; his mother, brother, and the kingdom, too. With his small entourage which had survived the darkness created by Ram's arrows, there was no place left to go back to, except to his motherland.

He had walked many miles to reach the palace, only to be turned away from the palace gates because the palace guards couldn't recognize him. In the olden days, the guards at the gates would have been executed for committing such an offence. But he understood that the blood clots, oozing pus, unkempt beard, and his torso covered with filth didn't automatically categorise him as the royalty.

"Inform someone from the royal household. Mareech is waiting at the palace gates," the *Rakshasha* said in a hoarse voice. It seemed he desperately needed some rest.

The guards guffawed in return. "You are standing before one. I am Vibhishan," one of the guards answered.

"And I am Ravan," the other mocked, flexing his biceps.

A *Rakshashi* standing next to the guards walked vivaciously towards the guest and ran her fingers coyly across Mareech's chest, making sure she missed the pus covered wounds. Sucking in her stomach which magnified her breasts, she whispered in a seductive tone, "Queen Mandodari at your command. I hope you will enjoy my company."

The *Rakshasha* reached for the female's mouth with both his hands. He slid his right hand inside her mouth which had been busy laughing at her own joke. Holding her upper jaw with the other hand, he brutally yanked her lower jaw down. In a few seconds, the force cracked her skull open. The *Rakshashi* fell unconsciousness, bleeding profusely. Her colleagues stood wide-eyed, unable to respond to the horror they had just witnessed.

"Inform Ravan that I am waiting," the *Rakshasha* repeated in a commanding voice that befitted a prince. The guards, shaken from their reverie, ran towards the royal court, and in no time, the prince was ushered in.

"Who did this?" he roared as soon as he saw his uncle.

"Vishvamitr," said Mareech.

'Changing your name won't hide your identity,' thought Ravan about the sage. He tried to remember what he'd looked like during his early years.

"But he gave up using weapons a long time ago," said Ravan referring to Vishvamitr.

"His students, Ram and Lakshman. They are the princes of Ayodhya," said Mareech.

Ravan hadn't heard of those names. He searched his mind trying to remember who the ruler of Ayodhya was, but it didn't ring any bells.

"How is Subahu? How is Tadka *ma*?" Ravan asked worriedly. It was only a few days ago that he had dispatched an ambassador to Tadka *van* with a message for the queen, his grandaunt.

Mareech broke into a sob and nearly lost his balance. Vibhishan left his seat and ran to console him. By then, his uncle was on his all fours, shaking and bawling.

"Both are dead," said Mareech in a broken voice.

Ravan couldn't believe his ears. Someone still had the courage in *Bharatvarsh* to challenge him directly. Tears formed in the corners of his eyes on remembering Tadka *ma*. All the childhood visits to his mother's home suddenly flooded his mind. As a child, he had played on her lap and she'd treated him as her own. Once he had assumed the throne of Lanka, he had sent her along with her sons, Mareech and Subahu, to establish their hegemony in the northern lands. Her success had dazzled many. Tadka *van* was counted as one of the most dreadful jungles around *Bharatvarsh*. He shook his head in disbelief.

"We need to meet Ram and his family," he said, dismissing the court of the day with a wave of his hand.

***

Ram rode with his newly wedded wife, Sita, towards Ayodhya. Vishvamitr and Lakshman followed the couple. It was a few days' journey.

Sita was scanning the surroundings with glazed eyes. Before commencing on their journey from Janakpuri, she had changed into something more comfortable than what she had been wearing at her wedding. Her father had wanted to send an entourage with the bride and the groom. As was the custom, he suggested the couple could ride in a palanquin which would be carried by the Videha's soldiers to Ayodhya. But Sita insisted on riding a horse.

"It would be quicker," she said, taking the reins of the horse in her hands.

"It will be a long way for you two to go," said Vishvamitr addressing the duo, "There would be many difficulties but make sure to overcome them together." Sita nodded reverentially, looking towards the sage who was riding behind her. The words of a *Brahmarshi* could not be taken lightly.

"Together," Lakshman guffawed looking at Vishvamitr, "Count me in, as well, master. At least one civilised person visited Videha today. They must be wondering what kind of a son-in-law they had chosen for themselves. On the very first day, he broke the most auspicious thing they'd possessed."

Ram was reminded of the parchment he had safely tucked in his rucksack. Taking care to ensure nobody noticed, he pulled out the folded piece of paper. In dark letters was scrawled a name everyone abhorred.

"It was the bow of Shiva. Whatever is written on this must be of utmost importance. Can I see it?" asked Sita. She had moved her horse alongside Ram.

Ram handed over the parchment. Sita read it and stared at Ram for a while. Like her husband, she was unsure about how to react. On the parchment, penned in neat handwriting in large thick black letters, was written a single name, 'Ravan.'

Sita pressed her palms together reverentially, looking towards the sky, and invoked Shiva's name in her heart, "You know him already, and he knows you now. You are the chosen one," she said.

ACKNOWLEDGMENTS

- 212 -

Arpita, my wife: for being patient and allowing me time to keep working on the book.

Meera RamPrakash: For being the most supportive editor one can find. Many more collaborations to come!

Umang Goel: Thanks for the illustrations. Couldn't have expected more.

Pallavi Mall: For pre-reading my work again and liking it. Her praises keep me motivated.

Akhilesh SV: My ex-roomie. A lot of tinkering of the storyline could be attributed to him.

And finally, thanks to *Bharatvarsh* - my *Matrubhoomi*, a land of billion lives and zillion dreams. It is only here that 'The Cipher of Kailash' could have taken place.

9 788819 377155 6